By My Nature

by

Bob Hatfield

By My Nature
Copyright 2006
by
Bob Hatfield
Cover design by Renny James
ISBN 1-932196-77-3

WordWright.biz
WordWright Business Park
46561 SH 118
Alpine, TX 79830

Printed in the United States of America

All rights reserved. No part of this book may be reproduced or transmitted in any form by any means, electrical or mechanical, including photography, recording, or by any information or retrieval system without written permission of the author, except for the inclusion of brief quotations in reviews.

Dedication

I dedicate this book to my wife, Francis. She remains my motivation, critic, and mainstay. She saw most of the events that inspired these tales and shares with me an appreciation of nature that borders on reverence.

Introduction

Real life made these stories. I saw them. I heard them. I lived them. I have veiled them in fiction. Liberally fictionalized, they stand typical of what can occur in a territory where primeval nature remains attainable in a few areas of the public lands of Oregon.

We remember a day spent in the pursuit of fish or game. Camaraderie around an evening campfire makes that memory a treasure. But the retelling of tales around that campfire yields something beyond price.

On the Genteel Art of Fly Fishing

I surveyed my storage shed in dismay. The contents of two large fishing tackle boxes lay in assorted groupings that covered most of the eight by twelve foot plywood floor. I had sorted, sharpened, or polished line, hooks, lures, flies, swivels and spinners and they awaited storage in two freshly cleaned and multi-compartmented tackle boxes. Scratches and wear-sign on several lures brought back favored memories as I stowed away the aggregate result of my life-long search for that perfect lure. I had enough gear to stock a small fishing tackle shop but many of these items had produced the sudden shock of a strike and a pole-bending, line-stripping battle with a good fish. I just knew the non-producers would give good results at some future date. The process reminded me of cleaning out an over-filled wallet; virtually everything goes back in and the familiar hip-pocket bulge remains.

I awoke from my reverie with the realization that nine a.m. lurked perilously close. By nine in the morning, Denny escapes his long-suffering mother (warden) and launches his curiosity at the local citizenry. Actually, Denny is an immediately likeable eight-year-old, keen witted and ingratiating but with a propensity for the bizarre. I can only imagine that things unbroken cringe in trepidation at his approach. One of his morning tours found me weeding my small vegetable garden. His eagerness to assist me resulted in the loss of most of my onion sets.

"Whadda ya doin'?"

The unmistakable voice of Denny Wharton propelled me to a rapid completion of my task.

"Rearranging my tackle boxes," I answered.

"I wanna help."

"All finished." I closed the boxes and secured the latches. Denny watched with intensity as I sat on the steps and unlaced my shoes in preparation for testing a new pair of waders.

"You got funny lookin' shoes and pants," he observed as I adjusted the suspenders.

"This is a new pair of waders," I explained. "I wear them when I go into a stream to fish."

"I just go barefoot," he said as if to imply I had wasted sixty- three dollars.

A few years prior Denny had eluded his mother's vigorous after-bath toweling and led her on an extended chase through the neighborhood while he stood barefoot all over. Satisfied at the comfortable fit of my waders, I picked up my fly rod and flexed it just to make sure that the great action I had long cherished remained.

"That pole wiggles so much it almost looks broke," Denny observed.

I ignored his evaluation, mounted a reel on the fly rod and threaded line through the eyelets. A few practice casts around the yard would reassure me that I stood ready for opening day of fishing season. I couldn't resist tying on a large buck tail fly just for realism.

With my left hand, I stripped line from the reel while my right arm moved in rhythmic arcs until I had forty or so feet of line traveling back and forth on a graceful circuit in preparation for placing the fly on a target clump of grass. My final stroke of the figure eight motion provided enough centrifugal force to avoid a whip action that could snap the fly off its leader. I then increased my exertion on the forward cast by just the amount necessary to present the fly on target. The bucktail flew with unerring trajectory to embed its barb in the back of my cap. I stood with line draped from my shoulders and steeled myself for Denny's words

"Are ya gonna try again?" Denny asked.

I thought my next several casts looked like textbook presentations of the fly (though only of moderate distance). Target tufts of grass fell victim to my expertise as Denny listened dutifully to my monologue on the genteel art of fly-fishing. His rapt attention dissolved into giggles as I snagged a rose bush on a backstroke.

"What a great cast," he chortled. "If we just had a few flying fish around here."

While I retrieved my fly from the rosebush I noticed Carrie Minton across the street. She kneeled in a flower-bed-tending position on hands and knees with head cranked around so that her line of sight fell across her own posterior to rivet on my activity. When our eyes met, she turned away quickly and entered her house. A gap of several inches appeared in her Venetian blinds just after her door closed. George, her husband, didn't have the couth not to stare at his neighbors, he watched me with frank interest as he peered over an azalea bush.

"If they want a show, I'll give them one," I muttered as I stripped line and worked my rod for the best cast of the day.

On the final forward thrust, the line played gracefully on a soft following breeze, and the leader line straightened to settle the fly at the base of a blueberry bush in the fence corner where a large, black cat pounced on it. The injured feline lifted his front paw and looked quizzically at the imbedded hook, then shook his forelimb vigorously in an attempt to dislodge it. Denny watched open-mouthed, George Minton shared Denny's shock, and wife Carrie stared in unabashed horror from an open door.

I had witnessed the insect hunting stalk-and-pounce technique of that particular cat on numerous occasions and knew him as a more than half-wild old Tom that bolted when approached. I had no desire to inflict injury and felt duty bound to somehow free the creature. I retrieved slack line with the reel as I started a slow approach to the cat, admittedly at a loss for what to do when I got there, if I got there.

True to form, the cat bolted in a frenzied, three-legged dash, yowling each time his tender paw touched the ground. His wild flight used up slack line quicker than I could strip more line from the reel and he hit the end of a taut line in a screeching flip that put a sudden and serious rainbow in my fly rod and reversed his course. He ricocheted off the chain-link fence, and then shot past me in a black streak that ended some fifteen feet above the ground in an apple tree.

"Boy, I like this." Denny had found his voice again. "I've always wanted to go cat-fishing."

My black antagonist hissed and spat as I reeled in line and neared the tree. His attitude left no doubt that he would not see me as the Good Samaritan

"This one's a real battler," Denny observed. "Do you want a dip net or a gaff?"

I aimed my most stern look at the youngster to no avail.

"Just how much does a fly-bug like that one cost?" he queried while pointing a forefinger treeward.

I stood, thoroughly perplexed, rod tip skyward and slack line retrieved, rapidly dismissing each solution that came to mind as either too risky or just plain impossible. Then the sheriff's car stopped at my front gate.

I pondered the number of laws I was undoubtedly breaking as Deputy Sam Wilkins walked up, but relief flooded me as he offered me two tickets to the annual Sheriff's Charity Ball. I could sense the knowing nods from across the street.

"How's fishing?" Sam quipped as I dug inside the waders to reach my wallet.

"Just taking a few practice casts," I replied as Sam's eyes followed the rod and line to the cat.

Sam sucked on a tooth and evaluated the entire scene. His eyes kept shifting back to the waders as if trying to justify my wearing them while practice casting on grass that wasn't even damp. As I paid for the Charity Ball tickets, I knew what my audience must be thinking: "He's going to bribe his way out of Class One Cat Poaching."

All of a sudden Sam got antsy and I could tell he didn't want to be invited to help in solving my dilemma. When his radio emitted a static filled squawk, he moved quickly toward his cruiser.

"Gotta go. That call's for me!" He spun a little on the gravel as he hurried away before bothering to determine the direction of the urgent call to duty.

"How are ya gonna get him down?"

"Let me think on it a bit. That cat's taking a break and I would like to do the same," I replied.

"Why dint'cha have Sam shoot him down? That way you could get your fishin' bug back."

At my urging, Denny made the short trip to my storage shed and returned with a lightweight aluminum ladder of four feet height and a machete. If I could get within a few feet of the skittish feline, I could chop the leader that draped across a limb and free the animal without his trailing a possible entanglement.

I stood on the second step of the ladder when an "Oh, My Goodness!" resounded in a shrill voice from across the street. "George! Go do something about that!"

The cat didn't seem to like the proximity of a machete-wielding climber any better than Carrie Minton did. He backed his way to the outer reaches of the tree snarling and spitting his objection to my invasion of his sanctuary. I stood at least ten feet from my objective when the nervous cat screeched his defiance and executed a prodigious leap from the tree that ended in an abrupt somersault two feet before ground impact as he hit the end of entangled line. I tumbled off the ladder to land butt first on the ground and looking at a suspended red and gray bucktail fly still twitching from sudden dislodgement. The barb had caught several black hairs.

The cat had vanished as a screeching black comet, and could still be running!

"Look!" Denny whooped. "You got your fishin' bug back."

I reasoned that since the hook had torn free, penetration had been shallow. Besides if that cantankerous old Tom could live through shredded ears and a score of battle scars, a number six trout hook would do no permanent damage.

Denny had stood quietly by during my inventory of personal injury from the fall. As I rose gingerly to an upright stance I reflected that retirement might prove more challenging than I had thought

Denny left me with some words of wisdom:

"It sure is gonna get hairy around here in September if you decide to practice for deer season."

Eventual Justice

Leroy Landrum, hopelessly addicted to the taste of venison and elk, also had a discriminating tooth that favored trout, salmon, grouse and quail. All of these delicacies abounded in the waters and hillsides near Florence, Oregon and Leroy harvested from this largesse to supply his table setting of eight. Nine years of marriage had resulted in six ravenous heirs and his wages as a plywood mill worker stood barely adequate to rear and provision his brood.

Summer weekends found him cruising coastal waters in a boat of sixteen feet, fishing for salmon and crab or sloshing through the mud of tide flats to dig clams. What they didn't eat during the week, they canned, smoked or froze along with wild berries and mushrooms for winter fare. The whole family stocked the larder, and Leroy headed up the harvesting while his wife ran herd on the preserving and freezing. Older children helped by cleaning and packing jars for the canner while the younger ones scurried to pick up clams that Leroy dug. The family employed three large upright freezers to stock their annual requirements. Jars filled the pantry shelves

This idyllic hunter-gatherer life style had a hitch. Existing state laws specified that Leroy should harvest nature's bounty during brief annual seasons. By contrast, his offspring required nourishment on a year round basis. Leroy overlooked the state's narrow-minded view. In short, Leroy existed as a poacher. Not one who exploited the local fauna for monetary gain, but to fill an existing need. This activity put him in direct opposition to Scott Davidson, a lifelong friend but unfortunately, also a game warden.

Scott and Leroy played together during elementary school and partied as inseparable teenagers as they honed their hunting and fishing skills. By the age of fifteen years, both had become accomplished hunters and good providers for familial table. It seemed that the game population increased in direct proportion to the distance away from the adjoining Landrum and Davidson homesteads. Even though creative in their interpretation of seasonal hunting schedules, they adhered to the principle of not killing animals not scheduled for table use.

Upon gradation from high school, the U. S. Plywood mill near Florence hired Scott and Leroy. Time not required for job or home duties remained devoted to the pursuit of fish and game. Their close relationship continued through courtship and early marriages but then came the bad news. Scott accepted state employment as a game warden. The appointment came as a major surprise to the local community in that it seemed akin to hiring a fox to guard the henhouse. Fortunately, Scott worked an area south of Florence and had no primary jurisdiction over Leroy's territory. Still, a cop is a cop, is a cop, as Gertrude Stein might have said.

Each out of season or over the limit critter came with a thought of what if. Worry came when Scott began working the Florence area during the month of March. At that time, mill workers were on strike and Leroy struggled to meet monthly payments and feed his hungry brood. It was a bad time for venison or elk that had shed their horns and entered calving time. Ordinarily he'd take a doe or cow, but it ran against his grain to do so during calving season. Leroy typified what the locals called a meat hunter, as opposed to the trophy hunter. He could appreciate a good rack of horns but his principle interest lay in harvesting an adult animal in prime condition for the freezer.

He lost several days in an unproductive search for fresh meat. Does seemed a no-no, and bucks kept to deep cover after shedding their antlers. Recognizing a smooth headed buck was easy for Leroy. Their wary nature and erect posture proclaimed their vanity but now they hid in deep cover until new antler growth re-supplied them with defensive weapons

The mill strike had a devastating effect on the Landrum family budget. Leroy augmented small meat market purchases with several grouse and a few brush rabbits, and then decided to try his hand at fishing. The state department of fish and game had just completed stocking area lakes with ten to twelve inch trout and the three largest of the lakes remained open for fishing year round.

A blown cylinder on his outboard motor placed a severe handicap on trying for trout in the larger lakes but he knew of a half dozen smaller stocked lakes of one to three acres. However, these smaller lakes and streams remained closed to legal fishing until the fifteenth day of April. This technicality gave short pause to Leroy before he cast a spinner into tiny Buck Lake and set about filling a stringer with rainbow trout.

Leroy didn't notice the white pickup truck until it came to a stop behind the trees that partially screened Leroy's own pickup from the view of highway traffic. The state fish and game logo on the doors brought a scowl to Leroy's face that slowly evolved to a wide grin when he recognized Scott Davidson as the driver.

"Thought you were working south of here," Leroy said as he hoisted a threshing trout from the water.

"This is a temporary assignment," Scott said, then added "You're getting a little careless aren't you? Fishing this close to the road before the season opens could be hazardous to your wallet."

"You oughta know. You've done your share of it," Leroy replied.

"Yes, you and I have drowned a few early worms together but this is a little different."

"Because you're wearing that monkey suit?" Leroy asked.

"No, because I pledged to uphold the laws that cover this situation."

Leroy's eyes showed more resignation than animosity as he looked at his lifelong friend. "I'm not out here just to get my kicks," he said. "Things have got a little tight during the strike."

"I can believe that," Scott said as he pulled a summons pad from a jacket pocket. "In a way, I'm glad I don't have an option about this. My supervisor sent me out here after he received a complaint by telephone."

A puzzled look came over Leroy's face as he took mental note of who lived nearby. "You mean to say someone actually squawked about my taking enough fish for a couple of meals?"

"It happens more often than you might think," Scott said as he tore a copy of the ticket from his pad and extended it toward Leroy. "I will explain your circumstances to the judge and I'm sure he'll fine you minimally with as much time as you need to pay." He then reached for the stringer of fish and added, "I am required to confiscate these fish too."

"I hope to hell they won't be wasted," Leroy said.

"No," Scott replied. "They will go to the County Juvenile Home or be donated to some other worthwhile project. Actually we are allowed quite a bit of discretion on final disposition. The one thing I cannot do is leave them with you."

Silence hung in the air like a deer fly as Leroy folded the ticket into a shirt pocket and set about stowing his fishing gear. Scott tried to brush it away with, "I'm sorry that I'm the one who was sent out here."

The following day both young men returned to a normal routine. The mill and the workers reached an agreement and Leroy went back to work. Scott investigated a possible deer-poaching occurrence. Both worried about how yesterday's events might affect their future relationship. Scott grew despondent that his duties had placed him in opposition to a friend and remembered his own indiscretions of the past.

Leroy accepted the inevitable had happened but it still stung that Scott presided over his demise. Scott found relief from bothersome thoughts as he set about impounding an out-of-season deer from a poacher. Leroy shifted his thoughts to the more pressing matter of providing for his brood during the two-week span before his next payday.

Scott's checkered past could reveal a multitude of fish and game law violations and successful evasions of legal repercussions, but he could still recall a tinge of conscience on each occasion. He found it difficult to accept these harsh restrictions on his favorite activities with quarry so abundant. He solved his dilemma the day he stepped behind a badge. His work now kept him in the natural environment he loved and he now enforced the law as diligently as he had once violated it. However, he realized his reformed convictions would be sorely tried if economic hardship endangered his providing for family. He chose not to contemplate this situation in depth.

The first day of Leroy's return to work found him performing the familiar steps of plywood production by rote. He reviewed events of the previous day as he flipped sheets of veneer into the gluing process. He felt anger at his cavalier attitude in fishing out of season within view from a main road. He harbored no animosity toward Scott and felt no guilt about fishing out of season. He regretted that he had placed Scott in an embarrassing predicament with no options. The upcoming fine would imperil a severely strained family budget.

All his various schemes to stretch his meager assets appeared to require the use of his hunting rifle in the nearby hills. One elk or deer would free up enough cash from the household budget to allow the purchase of fuel for his truck and possibly avert the crisis that threatened before his next paycheck.

A bounding four-year-old met Leroy on his evening arrival at his home.

"Come see," the boy said as he took his father's hand and led him to a garage door that stood ajar.

A deer carcass, cleaned, skinned and encased in a

game bag swung from a rafter. The attached note read, "We have considerable discretion in how we dispose of impounded fish and game...Scott."

A Dangerous Theory

Each weekend of the annual football season finds millions of Americans attending gridiron conflicts or viewing them remotely through the medium of television. Few of these fans consider the evolvement of this organized mayhem as anything other than an American phenomenon. Recent discoveries, however, have given rise to a theory that early versions of the game of football could date into Stone Age Europe.

The proposition that the hallowed institution of American football grows from foreign soil (however ancient) has triggered a mixed response from football enthusiasts. One faction, whether accepting or rejecting the proposal, found it only an amusing bit of trivia. The other group reacted with shocked indignation, which rapidly deteriorated into a stinging indictment of the theory and the mental stability of its originator. Soapboxes and radio talk shows became the preferred medium of choice for the rabid football disciples whose denouncements seemed well stocked with venomous adjectives.

Chief proponent of this controversial theory is

Percival Wiggins, Professor of Archeology at Weybeloe Normal, a small college in the Cascade Mountains of Oregon. A Cascade Clarion news reporter interviewed Professor Wiggins and wrote the following article:

Football...an Ancient Game?

Most people believe that the fall and winter madness of football that infects our land evolved from the English game of rugby. The first rugby match is thought to have involved rival fraternities at Eton. Students from Rugby witnessed the fracas, appropriated the idea and set about refining the game.

The first team at Rugby wore striped cravats and bowler hats, which they quickly discarded in favor of cardigan sweaters and padded stocking caps. Gentlemanly conduct prevailed until an unscrupulous headmaster awarded scholarships to outsized street urchins. A Queen's ban on the enrollment of uneducable waifs without proper lineage was deemed necessary to salvage the educational system. SAT scores sagged during this decade of unbridled recruiting.

Americanization of the sport came late in the nineteenth century. Several Ivy League schools experimented with the game of rugby. Various corrupted versions of the sport soon spread throughout the northeast section of the country. A plethora of serious injuries forced a standardization of rules and protective padding as the violent game grew in popularity. Weybeloe Normal, a small college in the Cascade Mountains of Oregon, has fielded a team for eighty-eight consecutive years. Percival Wiggins, Professor of Archeology and head football coach at the school, quarterbacked the nineteen fifty-six team that garnered Weybeloe's lone win in over seven hundred attempts. The visiting team played under a handicap in that they had eaten tainted seafood at a local inn the evening before game day.

Wiggins left a legacy to football fans with his comprehensive history of the game. Almost half of all shelf space at Weybeloe's library contains his research records and paraphernalia. A summer field trip last year took Wiggins and six undergraduates to Rugby and Eton in England, and then to southern France where they discovered cave wall murals that could legitimize a history of football into antiquity. One scene depicts eleven men in lion skins struggling to advance a cantaloupe-sized rock across a plain defended by eleven stalwarts in goatskins. Nearby slopes are packed with cheering spectators waving rabbit skins and raven wings.

A burial site in close proximity to the cave was long thought to contain war dead since all the skulls are cracked. Wiggins theorizes that these head wounds resulted from errant forward passing of the rock. Pictographs of a later era prove that an effective and less lethal passing game evolved when a dinosaur egg replaced the rock.

Most startling of the archaeologist's theories, he assigns to football the genetic improvement of the human species. Professor Wiggins believes that a well-played and stoutly contested game delighted spectators even in those early times. This theory receives some support from cave wall scenes depicting frenzied hillside bleachers in a state approaching mass orgasm as the egg advances through sectionalized pictographs. Since members of the losing clan coveted the wit and brawn of a winning team, custom held that to protect their honor, victors had to impregnate maiden relatives of the defeated squad.

This custom insured a gene pool to produce stellar athletes. Siegfried and Beowulf descend from this select breeding program. Children born of these gridiron unions fed on unicorn milk and prime rib of mammoth. Professor Wiggins plans an excursion to the Russian Steppes in June where he hopes to prove that the utilization of an inflated Siberian Tiger bladder revolutionized football by making it possible for a ball to survive for an entire game. The great quantity of dinosaur eggs destroyed during previous matches possibly contributed to the demise of these giant creatures.

The unexpected and controversial deductions drawn by Professor Wiggins from his research resulted in a withdrawal of financial backing by the National

Geographic Society and his disbarment from the World Association of Archeological Fellows (WAAF). *Sports Illustrated* picked up the tab for the June probe into the Steppes.

Art students at Weybeloe Normal are now creating a six-ton bronze statue of Professor Wiggins. The public flap resulting from Professor Wiggins' research has greatly helped Weybeloe's recruiting program. Four new members of the Junior Varsity squad have attended football contests as spectators. One nineteen-year-old freshman actually has game experience on the Junior High School level.

The expected upturn in advance ticket sales could provide for purchase of pads and helmets allowing the Weybeloe team to compete more strenuously with properly girded opponents. Letters to the editor denying possible European pollution of the revered American sport deluged the *Cascade Clarion*.

In responding to this flood of indignation, *Clarion* editor Hubert Blessing said that the article was a straight news story, not editorial opinion. He further noted that a game once popular with South American natives, circa seven hundred A.D., featured a stone hoop and rubber ball. This attempt to justify ancient sports brought a threat of defamation suit by the National Basketball Association. Students and faculty of Weybeloe Normal remained supportive of Wiggins' theories. However, a howling mob didn't share their views and burned the wooden goal posts at Weybeloe stadium. A college spokesman referred to the unruly group as fanatics and rednecks. The flaming goal posts ignited weeds in the end zone and only a timely mountain shower prevented flames from spreading to the log structure that serves as athletic dormitory.

A record sized crowd attended the first football game played in Weybeloe stadium after publication of the *Clarion* story. Spectators were evenly divided between those who ranted at Professor Wiggins for defiling American traditions and those who came to observe a team in action that had such an unbelievable won-lost record.

Twice referees halted the game in the first quarter to remove thoroughly ripened fruits and vegetables from the field. The visiting team departed by bus at half time and four schools in the Cascade conference telegraphed cancellation of contests scheduled for later in the season, subject to rescheduling after the resignation or demise of Professor Wiggins.

The professor/coach has requested re-negotiation of his coaching contract to include additional compensation for hazardous duty. A Weybeloe Normal College spokesman states that no salary increase will be forthcoming. The school does stand ready to provide a suit of Kevlar as protection against injury due to missiles directed at the coach during football contests. Negotiation on these conditions, however, might be a moot point as the entire football squad has petitioned the college to replace Coach Wiggins with someone having a more traditional outlook on football history and a practical plan for winning a game or two in present day competitions.

Wapiti Hoopla

Bubba Spencer reacted just as I expected when I told him I had invited Freddy Lee along on our annual elk hunt.

Distended neck veins and reddened face belied the soft voice as he hissed, "You're brain-dead!"

The previous eleven Novembers had found me accompanying Bubba into Oregon's coastal mountain range in the pursuit of Roosevelt elk. Bubba thinks of hunting as church. He has foregone weddings, funerals, gainful employment and sporting events during elk season.

Bubba's eyes stayed riveted on me as he took a long pull from his Budweiser can. "I don't want Freddy Lee in the same county with me during elk season," he said, and then added, "He's the only person I know that can create a two car traffic jam. Hell, he wouldn't know an elk from a unicorn!" His scathing indictment of Freddy Lee held much justification.

A three-point-eight grade average through high school and college gave testimony to Freddy Lee's academic ability but the young man remained woefully deficient in the art of everyday living. He had taken a position in his father's bank after graduating college with a degree in accounting, and stood as an asset in bookkeeping and auditing. His time as a loan officer didn't last long as the position required interaction with the public. For his lone attempt at becoming a jovial back-slapper, he received a broken jaw and cracked ribs. His stint as personnel manager ended when a maintenance employee with twelve years seniority quit in disgust following a two-hour lecture on how to clean and wax a floor.

I would never have chosen the arch-nerd as a fellow hunter, except that Frederick Leland Coats Senior, father and banker, intimated that including his son in our hunting plans just might enhance the status of my loan application. That proposal hit like a blow to my solar plexus but I maintained composure by concentrating on how desperately I needed a home improvement loan. I would have no peace in my abode until I converted the garage into a den and added a master bedroom and bathroom. I explained my predicament to Bubba.

He ground his teeth and asked, "Just how many privies do you need?" Bubba, a bachelor, did not know the agonies of sharing a single bathroom with a wife and teen-aged daughter.

In a desperate attempt to present Freddy Lee as an asset, I reminded Bubba that as a child he had been a crack shot with his air rifle. "He hit more cans and bottles than anyone," I explained.

"I know," Bubba agreed. "And now at age twenty-two he has graduated to shooting cans and bottles with a thirty-ought-six. Doesn't that seem like overkill to you?"

"He was on the ROTC rifle team in college," I countered. "He even competed in the William Randolph Hearst National Rifle Tournament."

Bubba sighed resignedly. "Mister Coats has spawned a perennial teenager. I have seen fourteen-year-old men. If he lives long enough, Freddy Lee will remain a fifty-year-old boy. He will never grow into being an adult, much less a hunter."

I pleaded until I got a conditional acceptance of Freddy Lee. I would baby-sit him at all times and be accountable for any faux pas in hunting etiquette. Further, I would ship him off to the meat locker with the first animal. Unspoken, but understood, was that we would move our camp while Freddy Lee ran that errand.

Elk season in Oregon always opens on a Saturday in mid- November. Bubba and I had agreed to meet Freddy Lee Friday afternoon in the Fisherman's Wharf parking lot. He arrived in his freshly waxed Chevy Blazer, the outsized knobby tires freshly blackened. A chromed light bar glistened above the windshield and a power cable winch topped the front bumper. Freddy Lee dismounted and stood wearing a broad grin as a radio antenna retreated into the fender well. His tailored shooting jacket matched the camouflaged pants that bloused into a polished pair of lace up boots. A broad brimmed hat, rakishly pinned up on one side and sporting a single pheasant tail feather topped off the ensemble.

"Hi, fellas," he beamed.

Bubba stared open mouthed. A Cabela's safari poster would pale in comparison. His gaze shifted to our spattered pickups, then to my scuffed boots and battered denims. He gave the splendored scene an apt appraisal as he softly breathed, "Gawda-mighty!"

Our small caravan climbed winding logging roads for twenty miles to our pre-positioned camping trailer. The hunting camp could have qualified for disaster relief. Our pickup trucks looked scarcely better than the ancient camp trailer. It had two boarded-over windows and a smoke stack jutted above the patched roof as evidence that a wood stove had replaced the original propane heating system. Bubba's watchdog, a large animal of confused lineage with outsized canines, was chained near the trailer's warped door. The fierce looking creature faithfully watched as people came and only left its prone position when offered edible morsels. A lone immaculate Blazer parked tentatively apart broke the uniform desolation of the scene. Perhaps a traveler had stopped momentarily to request directions.

Setting up camp consisted of no more than tossing

sleeping bags onto the two bunks and unloading a cooler of beer. A large box containing coffee, bread, beans, bacon, eggs and cold cuts completed the essentials of camp existence. I set about firing up the wood stove while Bubba nursed a can of Budweiser and watched through a grimy window as Freddy Lee attempted to ignite a campfire in the drizzling rain that had started to fall. As night closed in, Freddy Lee grew tired of striking matches and crawled into the elaborate nest of blankets he had fashioned in the rear of his Blazer. Bubba belched loudly and wormed his way into a sleeping bag. I followed suit.

Bubba and I drained a morning pot of strong, boiled coffee while Freddy Lee opted for a Pepsi cola and doughnut. We took both pickups. We left one truck on a logging road close to where Freddy Lee sat on the stand, and then Bubba and I took the other pickup in a circuitous route to the ridgeline. Our plan required each of us to come down adjoining draws that merged into a canyon one-quarter mile above Freddy Lee. The pickup left at the bottom served to retrieve the pickup on the ridge.

Areas of thick undergrowth punctuated the down hill hunt. Patches of salal and blackberry alternated with dense ferns. We slipped and skidded our way down slope to meet at the head of the canyon. Both of us had seen fresh elk tracks and droppings but had sighted no elk. As we caught a breather in preparation for the final quarter mile, the roar of Freddy Lee's 'ought six echoed through the canyon. A second shot came as Bubba and I split to opposite sides of the canyon and plowed our way through the brush, hoping to get a look at the herd that we knew was bolting our way or up steep canyon sides.

A third shot echoed out accompanied by the sound of breaking brush and slap of hooves. I hurried toward the racket of the bolting herd. Fifteen or twenty animals, each weighing between four and eight hundred pounds, are not difficult to hear when they panic. Trees and brush still prevented my seeing a single animal. I broke into a small patch of short ferns, thin trees and no brush. Evidence of the herd's exit upslope stood plain to see. Skid marks and plowed ground amid flattened ferns formed a trail that disappeared into uphill cover.

Bubba stepped out of the brush and stood looking at the torn-up trail. "Looks like someone plowed this up for planting," he observed. "Those elk are two ridges over by now; let's go see how the great white hunter has made out."

Freddy Lee wore a beaming smile and held a mangled soda can. "Thought maybe I should be sure my rifle was zeroed in," he explained. "Nothing to worry about though…it's dead on!"

I watched the disbelief on Bubba's face evolve slowly into rage and awaited the explosion of expletives that seemed imminent. When aroused, Bubba makes prolific use of an array of colorful adjectives. Yet, with measured stride, he walked quietly to Freddy Lee and took the can under scrutiny. "Yes," he agreed. "Your rifle is dead on, but you might consider a lighter load than that one-eighty grain slug. You tore that can up pretty bad." Without another word he walked to my pickup, hung his rifle in the rack and sat waiting for me to deliver him to retrieve his truck. Freddy Lee rode back to camp with me.

As we crawled into sleeping bags that night, I attempted an apology on Freddy Lee's behalf. Actually I felt responsible for the ruined day.

Bubba cut me short by saying "Freddy Lee can't help being Freddy Lee. I'm just sad for tomorrow."

In the pre-dawn of day two we moved over a couple of ridges for another try. We positioned Freddy Lee at the bottom end of an apple orchard on an old homestead site. After sweeping the area of cans, bottles and other tempting quarry, I advised him on the necessity for quiet concealment and set out for the ridgeline with Bubba.

Our second hunt took us down an only moderately steep hillside covered with young fir trees of four to six inches in diameter and referred to by loggers as Re-prod. Federal law requires timber companies to replant after logging off the original or second growth trees. Underbrush didn't stand as thick as on the previous day. We could see a good thirty to forty yards. We proceeded slowly, separated by seventy to one hundred yards, in an effort to spot the elk before they spotted us. The branch bulls we hoped to see (three or more points on each side) usually kept to themselves and away from the herd of cows and calves.

We spotted a feeding herd midway through the hunt and inched forward, making use of what cover stood available in an attempt to find an animal with horns. I had looked at six or eight slick heads when I saw a branch bull flash across a small clearing that lay ahead and to the right side of the herd. The viewing proved too brief for a shot. He wasn't spooked into headlong flight but traveling at a stiff-legged trot toward a point ahead of and down hill from the herd. I felt certain the herd's size was greater than the few I had seen. All elk within my view broke into that same stiff legged gait and moved toward Freddy Lee. I continued trailing the herd another ten minutes without catching sight of them again.

As I continued walking and hoping, two shots sounded from below. After a brief pause two more shots, pause again and one final report. I jumped behind a pair of closely spaced trees when I heard the elk coming toward me and away from the explosions below. I had a good look at five but saw no horns. One cow sped by within ten feet of me, mouth agape and hooves pounding.

I walked into the old homestead clearing to find an elk with long spiked horns lying in a heap, shot through the neck. Bubba came into view and stopped to view an almost identical spike only twenty yards from the first. We met at mid point between the carcasses.

Bubba spoke first. "Freddy Lee is your loan ticket, not mine. You get to tag one of these critters...nobody shoots my elk for me!"

Freddy Lee called out from the lower end of the orchard. "Down here fellas'... the best one is down here."

"I can't believe this is happening," I said.

"I can believe it," Bubba countered. "This has been the most bass-ackward elk season I have ever known! I'm living in a nightmare."

We stood looking down at the third animal, a heavy bodied bull with five ivory tipped points on each side of his rack. His palomino body coloring darkened to black on the mane and head; his heavy rump shone a soft yellow. Such an animal should delight any hunter but I only felt numbness. A mere three hours into the second day of the season and our planned week of elk hunting ended. The end result of a year's hoping and planning lay scattered around the old orchard and I had not fired a shot. Freddy Lee's high-pitched voice deepened the gloom as he recounted his recent exploits and anticipated how much fun it would be next year.

"There's work to do here," Bubba declared as he produced his elk tag and skinning knife.

We set about skinning and quartering the three animals. Freddy Lee's determination to assist in the process slowed things down considerably but by late afternoon the meat lay tarped down in the bed of my pickup.

Bubba seemed full of surprises that day. He clasped Freddy Lee's hand and congratulated him on a good exhibition of shooting, then turned to me and said, "I will phone the locker and tell them you are on the way with this herd. We can come back tomorrow and break camp. If you want me tonight, I will be at home with a jug of bourbon."

Freddy Lee followed me to the cooling locker where the quarters would hang for six days, then be processed and wrapped for freezing. He kept up a steady line of chatter while we unloaded and declared again his readiness for the next season.

I couldn't resist a parting shot. "I don't know, Freddy Lee. I've considered giving up elk hunting and getting into something else…perhaps photography."

Freddy Lee's shrill voice still yammered away as I mounted my pickup. "I have a dandy thirty-five millimeter with zoom lens and a cam-recorder and…."

Ophiophobia

The snake provides a marvelous example of nature's engineering expertise. A lithe body gives this predator access to the smallest crannies and burrows; hinged jaws allow for ingestion of a meal several times his body's diameter. Locomotion by legless gliding and subtle camouflage enable the snake to either ambush or stalk with a high degree of success. A speed-blurred strike followed by venom injection or strangulation by constriction leaves small hope for prey-sized animals caught within the strike zone of approximately two-thirds the snake's body length. Animals too large for serpent dining, place themselves at risk if they come into close proximity with a poisonous snake and trigger its defense mechanism. I realized at an early age that I fell in the at-risk animals category.

Some fail to appreciate the grace, beauty and pest-control value of the snake as expounded by herpetologists. They view the snake with mistaken fear, often abhorrence. Ophiophobia (fear of snakes) develops from early exposure to macabre folklore telling of hoop snakes with tail stingers capable of wilting an oak tree and milk snakes with appetites to bankrupt a dairy farmer. Serpents of outlandish size and possessing demonic powers abound in the repertoire of the tale-spinner. My own misgivings about the innocuous quality of reptiles originated in pre-school Bible class where I learned of the Creator's own admonishment of the serpent following the Garden of Eden apple incident. The phrase about striking man upon his heel stuck with me pretty good. I have great empathy for those people whose knee-jerk alarm at snake encounters remains an unshakeable faith. As a practicing member of that congregation, I fear for my heels in many a woods walk.

The contiguous forty-eight of these United States provides a home to a variety of non-poisonous snakes, such as the bull, king and garter. However, you can find four types of poisonous snakes: rattlesnake, copperhead, cottonmouth and coral. The fishing and hunting trips of my youth produced many snake encounters, causing me to realize my need for immediate classification ability. As I recall, snake sightings seldom occurred at a comfortable distance but virtually underfoot. My automatic reflexes at some of these surprise encounters produced leaps of Olympic quality.

Rapid identification presents its own problems. Poisonous snakes have triangular heads and blunt tails while the harmless types usually have elongated heads and more tapered tails. The rattler, copperhead and cottonmouth known as pit vipers, have deep pits on each side of the head between eye and nostril. These pits, highly sensitive to radiant heat, enable the viper to identify warm-blooded prey in the dark. They also have an evil vertical, black slit in the eye, while non-poisonous snakes have a rounded pupil. My encyclopedia states this as a fact, but I have never gone eyeball to eyeball for positive verification. The hemolytic poison of these particular serpents can kill prey-sized animals, and sometimes as large as cattle or humans. In short they can dissolve your blood, which the Bible and Mr. Renfield say is the essence of life.

The coral snake is slender and less than three feet in length with bright red, black and yellow bands circling the body. A harmless garter snake has similar markings but arranged differently.

A little poem proves effective in dealing with colored bands. It goes, "Red next to black, poison lack; red next to yellow, dangerous fellow." The coral, a member of the Elapidae family, also includes the cobra. It does not have the large fangs of the pit vipers and does not deliver its nerve-toxins via the strike. However, when touched, it will bite repeatedly. The coral lives in the southeastern states with one variety extending westward through Arizona.

The cottonmouth water moccasin has a thick body of chocolate brown to olive coloring with black transverse markings and inhabits swampy regions of the southeast and central United States. Normal adult length is four feet. Usually slow moving, it can deliver a speed-blurred strike at any animal that disturbs it. The cottonmouth gets its name from the stark white interior of its mouth, which it displays when it feels threatened.

The copperhead lives primarily in rocky or hilly regions from Massachusetts to Florida and westward to Illinois and Texas. Brown or pink-brown body coloring with darker brown blotches (often hour-glass shaped) provides effective camouflage for ambush style hunting. Though not normally aggressive, it will strike when stepped on, cornered or disturbed. The copperhead vibrates its tail rapidly but soundlessly as it lacks the rattle appendage of the rattlesnake.

Most vilified of serpents in snake yarns and folklore is the rattlesnake. One or more of the seventeen species of rattlesnakes dwells in each of the lower forty-eight states. The horned rattlesnake, commonly known as the sidewinder, lives only in the desert southwest. Smallest of the rattlers and one of the most aggressive, it seldom reaches more than thirty inches in length.

The timber rattler ranges from Maine to Texas and can grow to four feet in length, rarely more. Most numerous are the diamondback species, varying in color from gray to mottled shades of brown with large diamond shaped patterns along its back. The western diamondback ranges from Texas to southern California and can attain five feet or more in length.

The eastern diamondback, largest of the rattlesnakes, and therefore most terrifying, lives primarily in the southeastern United States, especially in the Florida Keys. It can reach seven feet in length and up to fifteen inches in circumference and has been known to exceed thirty pounds in weight. It is one of the most dangerous of American reptiles because of its copious ejection of venom and its aggressive nature. I consider myself lucky to have never met an eastern diamondback, and I hope this lucky streak will hold.

Rattlesnake venom, as with all pit vipers, contains at least two protein based substances. One depresses heart and lung performance and the other a histolytic, or tissue-disintegrating agent. Since the poisons are protein by nature, any coagulant, such as potassium permanganate, formaldehyde, chromic acid or heat, renders them less effective and provide a remedy for bites.

I have the identifying features of poisonous snakes indelibly etched in my memory, but my evaluation process kicks in only after I perform a reflexive leap to a safe distance. I will not stir dead leaves to expose the camouflage of a copperhead or determine the color arrangement of body bands that might possibly reveal a coral snake. Then too, who stops to check for a white palate on the cottonmouth whose body coloration resembles the harmless bullsnake.

The rattlesnake, given time, will sound a warning before striking. However, they can reverse this order if surprised. After considering the variables and dire need for speedy identification, I have reached an axiomatic conclusion: If it doesn't rattle it's a cobra!

When I identify a non-poisonous snake at a distance of ten feet or more I can rationalize the value of the creature in the control of rodents and garden pests. However, when I discover harmless little squirmers in a handful of weeds I have pulled from my garden, instant panic sets in. The split instant between sighting and classification wrecks the psyche and threatens heart rhythm.

Snakes have their rightful position in the orderly process of nature. Most snakes will devour any living animal that their distended jaws will stretch around, thus aiding humans in vermin control. The king snake does this too but takes the benevolent process still further with its cannibalistic dining preference for other snakes. In my opinion, this meritorious conduct qualifies the king snake for priority status on a protected species list.

A friend once suggested that I accompany him on a rattlesnake roundup. I declined his invitation, realizing that if we looked for rattlesnakes, we could possibly find them. His promise to do all the catching and handling while I carried a sack containing the venomous captives failed to entice me. The prospect of an after-round-up banquet of rattlesnake steak found me with no appetite.

Once, while hurrying along a short cut through a wooded area, I came upon a snake that spanned the narrow trail. It had a large girth but indeterminate length as head and tail lay concealed in low brush and grass. Prudence dictated a detour. Yet another serpent barred my new route. I backtracked slowly and left the infested area for the safety of an asphalt road. I arrived at my original destination ten minutes late but still managed to fulfill my role as best man at a wedding.

My little anecdotes only add to the bizarre serpent stories already in existence. I find myself in distinguished company, as classic Greeks didn't like the Hydra, and the English had a distinct dislike of St. George's Dragon.

If it doesn't have legs, I choose to avoid it. Then too, a garden just isn't a garden without a few bugs and slugs.

The Maturing of a Fisherman

A soft rumble of rubber on gravel did little to disturb early morning quiet as a pickup came down the drive and parked at the front of Mercer Lake Resort. The driver slid from his seat with a deliberate care born of advanced arthritis and many birthdays. He held the door open as a small boy bounced to the gravel on spring-like legs that came from his vigorous age of six years. The old man closed his pickup's door quietly so as not to disturb the vacationers that slept in resort cabins, then handed two spinning rods to the boy and carried a large fishing tackle box himself as they walked slowly down stairs that led to a dock. They paused briefly before boarding a boat. The old man had fished Mercer Lake for forty years and on each occasion he had paused to let his eyes rest on the scene that lay before him.

Mercer Lake boasted three hundred seventy acres of surface water over depths of up to fifty feet. Steep hillsides with towering fir trees entangled with undergrowth of salal, wild blackberry and rhododendron surrounded the lake. The three arms of the lake and several coves formed a meandering shoreline of eleven miles. Few visitors left Mercer without exposing a roll of film.

A soft grunt escaped the old man as he boarded the boat from a kneeling position. The small outboard motor started on the first pull; the lodge always kept the rental boats in top shape. He allowed the outboard to warm up at a fast idle while the boy ran back up the stairs to an equipment shed for life jackets and float cushions. He liked to watch the boy run. It looked so smooth and effortless. Once running was effortless for him too, and running had seemed so necessary.

Fishing began when the boat left moorage and entered open water. Some fifty to sixty feet of line trolled behind the boat at a speed no faster than a brisk walk. Each line held a short steel wire around which two small flashers spun when pulled through the water. They threaded a night crawler onto the hook that followed the flashers on a twenty-inch length of monofilament leader. What a great way to fish on an early May morning. They trolled parallel to the shoreline about fifty feet from the water's edge. Water depth in that area averaged twelve to fifteen feet. Lures ran six feet under the surface.

When a strike occurred on either rod, the old man shut off the outboard and reeled in his empty line while the boy retrieved the trout for him to net. He loved watching the boy during this action. He had set the reel clutch for proper tension and held rod tip high to let the limber pole absorb the trout's surges and jerks that could otherwise snap the six-pound line. The boy maintained a taut line at all times. The boy had learned quickly and remembered the old man's teachings well.

The old man insisted they keep only the fish they required for their table, all others they carefully released. They could legally keep five trout per person per day. Usually, they only kept six to eight fish as they fished often. Of course, the keepers necessarily included the largest fish of the day. Mercer, a natural lake, has a good population of native trout that the Oregon Department of Fish and Wildlife restocks every year with planters of eight to twelve inches.

The law requires a minimum length of eight inches but few fishermen keep fish less than twelve inches unless deep hooking or other injury makes survival unlikely. The state also imposes a further limit of one fish each day in excess of twenty inches. Abiding by that rule presents little difficulty, as enticing fish of such size to strike, and then to win the struggle that follows, happens rarely. A trout reaches that size only by successfully competing in an environment of constant predation. An average fisherman can easily take a limit of legal sized trout from Lake Mercer on a spring day except for the ones over twenty inches.

Two hours of trolling produced eight keepers that ranged from ten to fourteen inches in length. They returned several smaller fish to the lake. When they boated fish they placed them in a live box that ran the width of the boat under a hinged lid of the seat from which the boy fished. A continuous flow of cool water through the box preserved the day's catch in prime condition.

A necessary change in sitting posture and a frequent flexing of legs reminded the old man that his arthritic joints exacted a painful consequence for the time he spent with a thin cushion on a hard surface. He could no longer spend whole days in the boat, the pain-tax was too high. Yet, he sought no release from his lifelong addiction to fishing. The satisfaction that came from sharing the activity with his grandson amply rewarded his aches.

While trolling between fish they often spoke, usually in a question and answer mode. Two years prior, the boy's questions were a virtual mine field of posers such as, "What does the wind do when it doesn't blow?"

At the mature age of six years, the queries now focused on their fishing activities. Nostalgia and ambivalence weighed heavily on the old man during these periods, for he had heard these questions and caught these fish with his son thirty years before. That son had died in a logging accident shortly after his only child saw daylight. The old man felt grateful for his grandson, who provided the analgesic balm that soothed bittersweet memories; he also felt the responsibility of a role model. He and the boy formed an unlikely complement. One old and frail, one young and strong, yet each filled a void in the other.

"Old Tom could be round here," the boy said as his grandfather skirted a windfall fir tree that extended into the lake.

"Old Tom" was a legend-name they used when referring to a trout larger than any they had caught before. More specifically, it could denote any of several large trout whose fierce fighting had strained a rod or snapped a line before making their escape.

"Did my dad ever hook into Old Tom?" he asked

"Several times," the old man answered. "Once, I thought for sure he was going to land that fish but he lost him under the boat."

"I'll bet my dad would catch Old Tom if he could be here," the boy said in a pensive tone. "Or maybe no one will ever catch him," he added.

The old man winced inwardly and hoped that his grandson's ache for a father he had never known was less than his own for a lost son.

Stillness came over the boat. The boy lapsed into a familiar fantasy of how things might have been if his dad had lived.

The old man remembered what his own father had once said as he stood before an open grave, "No man should outlive his children. It's against the natural order of things."

The boy whooped and brought the old man back to

this time and space. The boy's pole arched and jerked rapidly and the reel clutch whined as line stripped off the spool. The fish turned suddenly and made a run directly at the boat, causing the boy to crank furiously to take in slack line. A spray of water exploded as the trout leaped through the surface and thrashed his head furiously in an attempt to throw the hook. Several more line-singing runs tired the fish until the boy led him alongside the boat to be netted.

Few creatures can equal the rainbow trout in sheer beauty. A streamlined and muscular body of near frictionless design allows swift passage through water. Duplicating the iridescent coloring from which the rainbow takes its name poses a severe challenge to an accomplished artist. Wide eyes and heavy breathing belied the boy's silence as he watched a spectrum of shifting colors that radiated as sun rays bounced off heaving sides of the fish.

"Thirty one inches," the old man announced after taking a measuring tape from his tackle box. "A trophy trout by any reckoning."

They had hooked the fish in a most fortunate way. The barbed point had penetrated the lower jaw so that the curved portion encircled tough cartilage and the shank extended out of the mouth. A deep hooking could have resulted in a severed line as tiny but sharp teeth sawed on the monofilament. The old man removed the hook and deposited the fish in the live box. They rebaited the lines and started trolling again before the boy broke his silence.

"I think I just caught Old Tom," he said, more in disbelief than elation.

"Maybe you did," his grandfather replied. "It's a good thing you caught him, that fish has lived long enough to die of old age."

The boy raised the live box lid and looked admiringly at the big fish for a third time. "Grandpa, does everything die when it gets old?"

"Yes," the old man replied. "That's nature's way. Some creatures have long lives, some not so long, but all life eventually ends."

"You are old," the boy blurted, a hint of anxiety in his voice. "Are you gonna' die?"

"Not right away, I hope." the old man said, "But it's something I can't avoid. Sooner or later it happens for all of us."

A light breeze from the northwest stirred the surface water signaling time to put away fishing gear and return to the dock. The wind over the lake usually intensified to produce small white caps by noon, not ideal conditions for old men or young boys

After they docked and tied up the boat the boy surveyed their catch for the day. "Two of these fish are dead," he said. "Six more are still swimming and the big one is just laying there but he's alive. Are eight fish enough for us to take home?"

"Sure," the old man replied. "What do you have planned for the other one?"

"I don't want Old Tom to die!"

"Grandma would like to see your big fish," the old man said. "But if you want to release him, she will understand."

The boy stepped back to watch as his grandfather netted the eight smaller fish and put them in a five-gallon bucket half filled with water. As usual, he'd add a few pieces of ice for the trip home.

"Are you sure you want to release the big one?" the old man asked.

The boy didn't answer but nodded in the affirmative.

"Well, it's your fish, so you release him," the old man said as he handed over the net.

The boy made several attempts before scooping up the still lively fish. He transferred the trout into the lake and then gently untangled it from the netting. Undulating fins suspended the big fish just beneath the surface as mouth and gills worked in tandem to extract oxygen from the lake. Forward movement began slowly, and then accelerated quickly as if sudden freedom had required a brief period of acclimation. They caught a final shadowy glimpse of the trout as he quickly faded from view with depth and distance.

The boy watched as the wake left by his trophy fish faded, and then died out completely.

It's for the Birds

I reasoned that by staking out a spring at the bottom of a canyon I could gain an advantage. I watched from brush cover as chukars glided down from rim rock and lit beside the small stream that trickled along the floor of the steep sided canyon. All the birds except one began their watering. One lone bird perched atop a boulder as sentry. I set about reducing the seventy yards that separated me from the covey. Stooping low and going slow, I took advantage of some streamside willows to get within twenty yards. I stood erect, twelve gauge at the ready, to see the chukars rock-hopping their way upslope some eighty yards distant. I sat down on the lookout boulder and gave loud voice to the ancestry of such obstinate creatures. This seemed to signal four birds that had for some reason remained behind to flush with a wild whir of wings. I scored two hits that fell into loose shale thirty yards uphill.

More than a little surprised by my good fortune I scrambled uphill to retrieve the birds and promptly slipped on the loose shale. As my ribs contacted a cantaloupe sized rock, the allure of a chukar meal lessened. I looked in vain for the bright orange feet of the birds. When I finally located my rewards, the colorful feet were tucked under camouflage feathers. I rump skidded my way downhill and thought of how a dog would have retrieved those birds far quicker than my half-hour effort and without rib damage.

Walking slow and taking shallow breaths I made my way back to my pickup. En route I watched another hunter approach his dog, which stood on point. When the birds flushed, the other hunter downed two of them as the covey scattered. One bird wheeled and came directly at me. That proved an easy shot and quick retrieve I would enjoy. That bird dropped within fifteen feet of my truck. I exchanged pleasantries with the other hunter and allowed myself an envious appraisal of his four footed companion. As I drove back to my camp trailer I renewed my vow to invest in a good bird dog on my return home.

I spent the next two days walking in corn stubble and alfalfa fields on irrigated farmland. The potato and onion harvests neared completion. Pheasants and quail ran plentiful in the brush that bordered these fields. The shooting remained good and I managed the daily limit of two pheasants and ten quail. I noticed that hunters with dogs got their birds with less walking and spent the late afternoons at taverns watching the world series of baseball while I sore-ribbed my way along irrigation ditches and fence lines for an occasional bird. I reasoned that the fresh air and exercise made for a healthier life style than lounging in front of a boob tube of baseball in a smoke filled tavern. The cool spring water from my canteen provided my only libation during hunting hours, but a cold Budweiser at sundown served to moderate my envy of the hunters that came canine-equipped. As I cleaned and prepared the day's birds for freezing, I had an ambivalent feeling of gratitude for the birds in hand and the urge to go back to the punishing pursuit of chukar. No amount of hard running allowed me to catch up with the phantom covey that haunted my sleep that night.

Dawn found me back in the canyon sipping coffee from a thermal cup and listening to the raucous rapid chukar-chukar-chukar assembly call of chukars in the rim rock. They also sound this call to reassemble after being flushed and scattered. As the chukar calls grew fainter, I reasoned that the birds were feeding uphill onto the sagebrush flats beyond the canyon wall and I determined to find an access road to that area.

A graveled road followed a small creek that flowed the nine-mile length of the canyon. I exited at the top end onto a sagebrush mesa that stretched toward more hills and canyons in the distance. I followed several faint roads to holding pens used by ranchers who ran cattle on a vast expanse of government grazing lands. Several times I saw chukars in the distance but could not get within shooting range.

The covey ran in their peculiar upright stance; nothing seemed to move except their blurred legs. They flushed as I approached gunshot range, flew fifty or sixty yards and glided to the ground with feet churning. It seemed that my feathered adversaries knew the effective range of my twelve-gauge

By noon, I had burned up a half tank of fuel, seriously degraded a good pair of boots and harvested exactly one chukar. My lone victim, an intellectually challenged creature, didn't flush on cue with the covey. I motored my frustration to a windmill fed stock watering tank and parked for a sandwich and soda.

A low whine interrupted my lunch. I looked out my open window to see a dog sitting erect and again heard the pleading whine. I pinched off a piece of sandwich and found bologna a canine favorite. Together, we finished the sandwich and I gave him a drink of melted ice from the cooler by pouring it into a hubcap. The dog evidently liked my way of building sandwiches for as I bounced my pickup along a faint trail through the sagebrush, he trotted alongside.

I had gone no more than two hundred yards when I saw several chukars cross the trail ahead within range of my Remington. I bailed out of the truck in time to pick off a single but the rest of the covey flushed out of range. The bird had scarcely hit the ground when the dog sped past me, picked up the chukar and brought it to me. The performance bordered on the unbelievable. That little pot-licker bore no resemblance to a bird dog. I tried to puzzle my way through his confusing lineage. No predominant breed characteristics stood out. I finally settled on his being a Heinz.... at least fifty-seven varieties seemed a likely blend.

I invited the mutt into the cab with me on the slim hope that he just might do it again. I drove to where the covey had settled and invited him to perform.

"Get 'em, boy," I urged. The dog cocked his head to one side and looked at me quizzically.

"Hunt birds," I said and pointed into the sagebrush. "Hunt birds!"

Being rather a bright little fella' the dog realized I expected something of him and sprang into action. He rolled over twice, yapped once and sat up erect on his rump. I repeated my suggestion that he hunt birds and got a different response. He brought me a twig for a round of toss and fetch. I looked at his floppy ears, short legs, long hair and pointed snout. He evidenced absolutely no kinship to pointer, setter or retriever. He wore a frayed and loose fitting collar but had no license or ID tags attached. No house stood within ten miles of our location. Since the mutt seemed to know simple tricks that a youngster might teach, I felt duty bound to take the animal back to the trailer park and try to unite him with his owner.

The shoot-and -retrieve routine repeated several more times on the return trip. A total of six chukars made that day my most productive. No one at the combination country store-post office could identify the dog so I bought a can of dog food and headed for the trailer park. As night closed in, the dog seemed content lying under my trailer beside the food and water dishes I had provided.

I awoke the following morning ready to share another sandwich and play the shoot and fetch game. The dog had left. I searched the trailer park and drove slowly along the highway and down the small town's one side street to no avail. I turned anxiously to the trailer park operator but he had no knowledge of any such dog. I recounted the events of the day before, realizing that any sane person would doubt their authenticity.

"You're the third guy to tell me this same story," the park operator said. "I heard it two times last year. Guess I'll have to start believing it."

I went back to the sagebrush flats and drove the length of the canyon but never found that little dog. For the past three years, I have been most careful of when and to whom I tell this improbable tale for fear I might acquire a label I don't particularly relish. I still don't have a well-trained bird dog, but I'm working at it. I have managed to get a pedigreed pointer pup to sit up for tidbits but retrieving a feathered training ball seems a bit complicated for him. A neighbor reasoned that the animal has the qualities necessary to develop into a good bird hunter if he can only find a trainer smarter then he is.

I'm looking forward to a return engagement with my feathered antagonists, accompanied by a bird dog. I know that I will relish each challenge and willingly endure long hikes through rugged terrain. I have high hopes for a good performance by the dog I'm attempting to train but will still stand ready to share my lunch with a phantom mongrel mutt that vanishes after getting a little love, maybe the one thing he didn't get a chance to retrieve the first time around.

My Process of Aging

The years rush on at an accelerated pace. I can remember that during my childhood there was an average of two years between school vacations and often times three or four years between Christmases. Such, sadly, is not the case now. Monthly billings from creditors seem to arrive on a weekly basis and a galloping calendar is loaded with birthdays.

In my youth, I often wondered if I might live to see the millennium, now a fait accompli. As the calendar made its big rollover, I had attained my three-score and ten. I often fancied myself an avid participant in the festive celebration that would take place on such a momentous occasion, replete with champagne, caviar and fireworks. Actually, my revelry on the eve of year two thousand consisted of orange juice, cookies and a book near a cozy fire.

The inimitable Mark Twain once made an incisive observation on the aging process. When asked by a young interviewer if he dreaded growing old, he replied, "Not when I consider the alternative."

On reading this, I remembered that near the end of my three-year army enlistment, a Colonel suggested that I pursue an army career to a twenty-year retirement at age thirty-seven. I declined his invitation by reasoning that at the advanced age of thirty-seven I would be too decrepit to pursue the many (though vague) great deeds I was certain to accomplish.

Recently a client questioned me about electrical capacity for equipment in his shop. I could not recommend a solution with certainty, so suggested that we consult an electrical contractor. I later marveled at age seventy how many things I don't know, for at the tender age of twenty I knew everything.

My current health status remains acceptable even if less vigorous than in younger years. I owe this in part to successful shoulder surgery, updated eyeglasses, dental partials, arch supports and a fifteen-year regimen of high potency vitamins with minerals. I've maintained a reasonable cholesterol level through a low fat diet and near elimination of eggs and dairy products. At times it seems that those things I desire most are illegal, immoral or at least a dangerous health hazard. It occurs to me that the "Golden Years" could be more accurately compared to brass that tarnishes quickly without regular polishing.

But back to Mr. Twain. Although known as a hell-raiser, he adapted his activities to his age limitations and enjoyed each stage of life to its fullest potential. I consider myself fortunate to have actively engaged in work, avocation and recreation to my liking. Many of my contemporaries have either assumed room temperature or have severely restricted regimens. I can still approach each day with a tinge of optimism and purpose. However, these attributes often diminish by mid-afternoon. After a days work I sometimes reward myself by remaining awake long enough to view the public channel news hour, which concludes at eight p.m., though I prefer a book to most TV fare. All things considered, life progresses acceptably. And, when I consider the alternative ...

Now to the crux of these ramblings. I progress toward my eventual reward (or possibly my arraignment). I don't feel that the event is imminent, but suspect strongly that it lays somewhere in my itinerary. Were it not a command performance, I'd just as soon forego my role at center stage. Through careful planning, and with luck, I might achieve a few postponements and hope for encore. No matter the date for my finale, I will approach final curtain with strenuous objection.

In reflection, I've had an eventful life journey. I have not realized some of the things I desired, but many wonderful things were given to me. I have tasted of success and failure, known exquisite happiness and deep sorrow. My pursuits have provided me with an adequate if not affluent life style. Some of my accomplishments I can view with pride, many of my failures bring regret. I have experienced tornado, flood and fire; these have let me witness the inherent good that can surface in people. Fishing and hunting have endowed me with an appreciation of nature that borders on reverence. I have lived to see my children firmly established with families of their own; for this I am grateful. Since becoming a great-grandfather I have considered emulating my great-grandmother Kimmell and hang around long enough to see the fifth generation but it is unlikely that I will attain such antiquity.

I find it more than a little awkward to possess a slowing metabolism while living in a fast paced society that continues to accelerate. My thoughts often digress to the slower pace and gentler times of my childhood. Since returning to that era is unlikely, I do the next best thing and maintain my residence in a rural setting. I departed Florence when that town got its third traffic signal and its population burgeoned to five thousand. A fourteen mile move brought me to Mapleton, which, with two hundred souls stands slightly too large.

A recent trip necessitated air travel. I felt my apprehension justified when I entered the mad house of Portland's air terminal. I am most grateful to the travel-wise friend who escorted me through that maze to a particular counter where I received a confusing stack of papers that turned out to be my ticket. My guide then deposited me in a line of people in moderate stages of undress attempting safe passage through a metal detector with varying degrees of success. I noticed that two of the petitioners were garbed in mid-east fashion and immediately remembered that a few people so dressed have demonstrated a rather bizarre behavior pattern toward aircraft.

"Run em through again," I thought.

My hopes for a sleek and modern jumbo jet faded as I boarded a nondescript Seven-Twenty-Seven older than many of its adult passengers. The worn upholstery and frayed carpet failed to instill confidence, but the old craft wheezed and clattered its way through take-off, then struggled skyward. The flight itself proved uneventful until we joined the near misses above Dallas-Ft. Worth International. Dozens of aircraft weaved their way through organized confusion toward ground safety. Jittery acceptance of my predicament gave way to controlled terror as our touchdown created a roaring vibration that suggested either flat tires or square wheels; my flatulence went without notice. The raucous wheel noise subsided as we rolled to an eventual stop.

The massive terminal seemed an endless complex of wide hall-like thoroughfares leading to infinity. Thousands lounged in adjoining waiting lobbies while thousands more scurried toward ticket lines, boarding areas and exits. Each of these people clearly were terminal-wise and knew exactly how to accomplish their purpose. I alone had my rudder askew. DFW added its final straw when I answered nature's call and searched in vain for a flush valve. When I stepped back to better survey the cubicle, the plumbing automatically activated. I retreated to the waiting area where my daughters rescued me to the comparative sanity of freeway traffic.

For my return flight, they deposited me at the terminal sans guide, and I quickly discovered that they cleverly conceal airport information desks and staff them with first-day trainees. However, the seasoned traveler that I am now, I negotiated the prerequisites and boarded a Seven-Thirty-Seven that, at least in appearance, instilled more confidence than the previous craft. The magazine I read in flight did not elevate my low esteem of air travel. An article indicated the possibility of an industry-wide structural correction on all 737s. I came out of the ordeal convinced that we can only obtain fail-safe flight with feathers.

Fear of short-term memory loss has neared phobia stage for many of my contemporaries. People interpret the inability to recall a name or telephone number as a symptom of Alzheimer's. This panic situation does not exist for me, as I have never possessed an outstanding memory. Even as a child, my ludicrous performance in this field led my parents to often let me hide my own Easter eggs. I have long maintained written notations of vital addresses and telephone numbers while relegating casual acquaintances to a grouping of whatshisface or whosits.

I welcomed the debut of tubeless tires, automatic transmissions and television, and then eagerly accepted the pocket calculator and cordless tools. Computers, however, have left me awestruck. Information that once took weeks of diligent research now appears instantly. Computers have either enhanced or invaded every aspect of my life. I deposit remuneration for my labor into a bank account via plastic and electronic funds transfer pays my creditors on schedule.

I sometimes never see the crisp, green legal tender that once heralded payday. Government, industry, finance and the baking of our daily bread rest on the silicon chip. Failure of these electronic marvels could drop planes from the sky and I'm already convinced that their suspension on thin air remains tenuous at best.

A late model computer now dominates one corner of my home. My wife took a community college class, and has grown moderately proficient in the art of electronic manipulation and now speaks computerese as well as her native English. She has upgraded my small construction business through computerization of estimates, proposals, billing and bookkeeping. For the present, I retain control of driving nails and pouring concrete. In spite of the obvious advantages of digital literacy, I still avoid our computer corner and view it with trepidation normally reserved for rattlesnakes. Just by depressing the switch, I might accomplish silicon meltdown.

Since each passing day diminishes my allotted time in this earthly plane, it occurs to me that I should view my cup as one-third full instead of two-thirds empty. By shifting gears and accelerating, I just might keep abreast of that vivacious and glittering parade of life that I first joined so long ago. I intend to board an airliner (fully expecting to reach my destination), and fly to Dallas, where my son conducts classes in computerese and electronic wizardry. I shall view the aging process only as a minor handicap worthy of my efforts at compensation. It holds no dread for me. "Not when I consider the alternative!"

First Buck

    Knobby tires sang on sun-warmed asphalt in harmony with muffled exhaust rumbles as a green pickup monotonized its way across Oregon's high desert. The long ribbon of highway undulated over gentle rises to disappear as a thin line on the horizon. Fourteen-year-old Michael Hatchett watched from his passenger side window as sagebrush on parched and rocky soil slid past in sameness like a repeating picture on revolving canvas.

    Michael's fourth year to accompany his father to eastern Oregon in pursuit of mule deer had finally come. Each trip had resulted in a large deer with a respectable set of antlers and he had assisted in the field dressing and hanging of each animal. A weeklong camping trip with his father stood out as the high point of each year for Michael. They cleaned all the camping gear and inspected it before packing. They treated the tent with water repellant, sharpened the axe and knives to keen edges and shopped for canned and dried provisions. Preparations even included extra home study assignments to prepare him for six days of absence from school.

This year would be the best. He could hunt, not just observe and assist but hunt as an equal with a hunting license, deer tag and his own rifle. Michael resisted the urge to turn and look at the gun rack that spanned the rear widow. Viewing the scene did not improve the indelible picture in his mind. The top set of brackets cradled his father's thirty-ought-six Browning with a new lever action two-forty-three Winchester slung below it, a parental gift to Michael on his fourteenth birthday. The gleaming newness of the lower weapon contrasted sharply with the brush scratches and worn bluing of the thirty-ought-six. Both rifles had three-to-nine variable scopes and leather slings.

Michael adjusted a wing window to ward off some of the desert heat and popped the tabs on a pair of sodas from a cooler at his feet. He passed one to his father and watched as Michael senior took a long pull from the beaded can. He liked watching his father.

Michael Benjamin Hatchett senior, a true mountain man, wished he had been born in another age. He stood an erect six feet tall and weighed one hundred ninety five pounds, with quick reflexes and good vision. For fifty weeks of each year he used his physical and mental talents to harvest, mill and market the Douglas fir trees of the central Oregon coast. He sat aside one week each summer for a vacation of his wife's choosing, and a remaining week for hunting deer in eastern Oregon. Black tailed deer ran plentiful in the coastal region but the larger mule deer of the high country challenged him more. Venison fed on sage and bitter bush then hung to cure in the thin, cool air of a high pine forest made premium fare for the Hatchett table. The family approached each winter with freezers well stocked with Oregon's natural bounty. They froze or canned wild blueberries, blackberries, mushrooms, quail, grouse, salmon, and garden vegetables. Weekend hunting in the low coastal mountain range usually produced an elk. Big Mike, as friends knew him, a good provider, worked hard and shrewdly at his small logging and milling company. He could have easily stocked family larder from supermarkets. Chicken, turkey or beef might be acceptable but they preferred pheasant, grouse or venison. They chose to be hunter-gatherers.

As the pickup up slowed for the town of Hines, Oregon, the Hatchett duo spotted the familiar, if incongruous sight of the large Hines mill and wood processing complex. After one hundred miles of open desert, the mill, its receiving yard piled high with pine logs, stood out in stark defiance of such wide expanse without a marketable piece of timber in sight. They swung north onto the Izee Road, across from the mill's entrance, and up a steep grade that wound its way through foothills and eventually into the pines of the Malheur and Ochoco National forests, source of the mill's timber.

Little more than an hour sufficed for them to arrive at the Sage Hen Springs campsite for the hunt. Here a two-inch stream of cold, artesian water had surged continuously from the base of a hill since its discovery by early trappers. Tall stands of pine trees grew interspersed with rock and sagebrush flats that fell away to spring-fed gorges. The area seemed further removed from a modern setting than the thirty-five miles that separated the twin townships of Hines and Burns from Sage Hen Springs. Ten paces off any forest service road could deliver an adventurer into a prior century.

Setting up camp followed a routine established on earlier hunts. They erected a domed nylon tent over a bed of straw from a bale in the pickup. Big Mike unloaded food coolers and camp gear while Michael removed dead ashes from a fire pit ringed by a twelve-inch wall of rocks, then cleared pine needles and wood debris within a ten-foot radius. He cut and stacked dried wood and laid a fire in the pit for evening lighting. A two-foot stump, three feet in diameter, served as a base for their two-burner propane stove. A propane lantern hung from a near-by limb. A pine pole, three inches in diameter was lashed across a six-foot gap between trees for hanging deer. They chained two sturdy cooler chests atop a stump to discourage any marauding animal that might wander through. With the camp ready for use, they devoted remaining hours of daylight to a scouting trip of forest service roads and spur logging roads.

Deer that had bedded down during midday began to stir and forage in the cool of early evening. Small groups of does with fawns and yearlings took only casual notice of the passing truck. Occasional spikes or forked horns stared intently, while larger bucks remained noticeably absent from view. Large hoof prints at two widely separated water holes advertised their presence. The largest set of tracks sank deep enough into mud at waters edge to allow dewclaws, situated at rear of the ankles, to leave twin punctures behind the hoof prints. So recently had the buck made the tracks that water still seeped back into them. Big Mike raised binoculars to view a belt of trees and brush that wound down the large knoll toward the water hole, then swept upslope to rim rock but he only saw a coyote that loped lazily into the distance.

Darkness ended their exploration and Big Mike eased the pickup down a bumpy fire cut and toward the main road. As headlights swept the final turn he braked suddenly. Father and son stared in silence at a large buck that stood statue-like, frozen in the headlights. A twitching tail provided the only movement for an eternity of several seconds, and then with one leap, only an empty road remained.

"He was big!" Michael breathed softly. "At least a three pointer."

"Four," Big Mike corrected. "And it always seems

to happen unexpectedly, in an unlikely place and before opening day."

Sleep came slowly to Michael that night as he mentally pictured how that big buck might look in the cross hairs of his scope. Things just couldn't get much better. Their previous trips had included several of his father's friends and Michael could recall every hunting story told at the campfires. This hunt, his hunt, would be the best of all. He had a new rifle, his first deer tag and time off from school to hunt and share it all with his dad.

Michael awakened to the smell of coffee and hurried his way through two cinnamon rolls. A full breakfast of bacon, eggs, and potatoes would come after the morning hunt. First light showed above the tree line as their pickup left camp. Michael got out at the same fire road they had traveled the night before and watched as taillights disappeared around a curve, then set out slowly down the barely discernible fire road. Big Mike circled to the rear of the knoll where they had seen the coyote and would hunt toward Michael for the mile or more that separated the pair.

First trees, then smaller brush grew distinguishable as Michael slowly worked his way down the road. He paused frequently to listen and to scan the ground ahead. He observed each opening in the trees and underbrush carefully before he left cover to cross exposed areas. He remembered Big Mike's admonition to hunt slow and quiet, into the wind and to make good use of cover. No wind stirred the morning chill but his slow progress paid ample heed to the rest of that advice. Michael considered all hunting suggestions from his father axiomatic.

Several times Michael saw does and their fawns browsing in the distance. On these occasions he kept to cover and viewed the slick heads through his scope. He scanned the brush line near these small groups for the amorous buck that might lurk nearby but Big Mike had said it still seemed a little early for rutting season. He noticed a slight movement in the brush and eased the cross hairs over to center on a forked horn. The little buck turned and looked directly into his scope from one hundred yards. Michael felt good about spotting him before he spooked, but a full week of hunting remained and the buck he had in mind stood considerably larger and would have a better rack of horns.

The morning sun started its climb above the tree line as Michael stopped to view a down-slope of sparse brush and scattered second growth pines. The water hole where they had found large tracks the day before lay some seventy yards away at the bottom of a wide but shallow draw. A thin belt of brush and trees that started at the water hole snaked its way uphill to rim rock a half mile away. He knew that Big Mike would come over the top within an hour and follow the brush line to the water hole. They would then circle the base of the knoll in opposite directions and meet at the pickup.

Michael sat on an old growth stump behind thin brush cover to watch for deer his dad might push his way. He knew that any buck attempting to keep ahead of Big Mike's progress would probably come down the belt of cover to get into the thicker stand of trees that lay across the fire road. Much of the area on Michael's side of the water hole lay open for a shot opportunity if a buck felt pressed hard enough to break from cover.

Big Mike made slow progress up the backside of the knoll, zigzagged as he took advantage of brush patches and outcroppings of large rocks to shield his movement. He had covered three quarters of the slope when he turned toward what sounded like a small rock clattering down from the rim rock area above. He glimpsed only the hindquarters of a deer as it went over the top. One quick look at the area under overhanging rim rock told a complete story. Small bunches of wiregrass lay flattened and deer droppings, old and new, lay scattered among hoof prints on ground loose and dusty from long use. It provided a perfect bedding area that offered concealment from above and a vantage point for viewing the area below through thin brush. A game trail led through a break in the rim rock and into the belt of vegetation that wound down the opposite side.

Occasionally a magpie's caw disturbed the stillness of the water hole, but mainly silence echoed in his ears, the best music, and the best overture for a hunt. Michel sat watching a doe with two fawns that had browsed their way down the slope, nibbling at bitter bush and pine seedlings. The sun felt warm on his back as it chased away the last of an early morning chill. A slight movement at the bottom end of the brush belt riveted his attention. He fought back the urge to lift his rifle and scope the spot. He sat in frozen silence, knowing full well that a buck in that brush would immediately spot any movement on Michael's part. A long minute dragged by before a gray muzzle and black nose showed briefly, then withdrew -- a deer, and from the wary attitude, possibly a buck. Does seem to realize they have little to fear in open areas. A buck, however, knows to be cautious. Michael knew that the animal must break left or right to skirt the water hole and cross the open area in order to reach the safety of thick cover that lay above the fire road. Doubling back uphill and sneaking past the pressure from behind didn't provide a safe option for the animal as the narrow belt of thin trees and brush wouldn't provide enough concealment, averaging twenty to thirty feet in width. Michael's exterior composure belied the tension building within him as he waited, finger on the safety catch and legs tensed. He did not know with certainty that the animal had horns; he had caught only a brief glimpse of the head in gnarled brush that offered confusing camouflage. The silence grew so thick that he unconsciously guarded the whisper of his breathing. The symphony would soon start in earnest.

Without further warning, the deer broke from cover, neck extended and hooves pounding. Michael snapped the safety catch and raised his rifle in one smooth motion as he came to an upright stance. The two-forty-three cracked in unison with a sideways lurch by the deer, followed by a burst of speed that carried the animal over the fire road before Michael could chamber another round and locate him in the scope. It shocked Michael that the deer had not dropped. Michael had had an open shot. He ran to where the deer had stood when he fired. As he searched the area for blood sign, he could picture the buck that had filled his scope and seemed to have horns all over the top of its head. He had gone no more than a dozen paces upslope when he found blood on a tuft of wiregrass. He could almost hear Big Mike's advice: "Follow at a walk. Don't run."

Larger blood splatters appeared during his progress uphill. As his plane of vision topped the rise, he spotted the buck crumpled at the far edge of the fire road. He approached slowly, rifle at the ready but the need for caution had passed. He looked down at the buck and for the first time saw a slight twitching in his hands. He swallowed hard against the dryness in his mouth. His first buck was not the behemoth that he had imagined, but nonetheless, a heavy bodied mule deer. The horns might not make the record book but they were a sturdy, symmetrical rack with three matched points on each side.

Michael took out the chambered round, refilled the magazine and propped his rifle against a tree. He took a plastic bag from his pocket and dropped it to the ground for heart and liver, then unsheathed his knife. He cut two tiny notches in the toe of a front hoof just as his dad had always done and kneeled between the buck's hind legs. Working carefully to avoid puncturing intestines, he set about gutting the animal.

Big Mike had barely started down the knoll when he heard the distinctive high-pitched bark of the two-forty-three. He stepped from cover and raised binoculars to his eyes. He watched as Michael searched the ground then started uphill. Lifting his focus higher, he could see the white rump and gray body of a deer. The woods hid head and horns but several tines flashed visible. He felt pride as his son trailed his first deer. He watched until the boy knelt to gut the animal, then lowered the glasses and turned to retrieve his pickup.

The smile on Michael's face told it all as he stepped toward the slowing pickup with rifle in one hand and the bag containing heart and liver in the other. He hung his weapon in the rack while Big Mike put the bag into a cooler, then they both went to where the deer lay. Michael tied his tag to the horn base with a string.

Big Mike laid a light hand on his son's shoulder.

"Clean shot on a good buck," he said with a grin.

They each gripped a horn and pulled toward the pickup. The first movement of the symphony was over, the second started with the sound of a Blazer on the fire road.

At first nothing seemed unusual about three men exiting a Blazer that stopped on the fire road, but when one of them tossed an empty whiskey bottle into the brush, a red flag went up for Big Mike. He didn't oppose the use of alcohol in moderation, but his interpretation of moderate use while hunting meant total abstinence. Michael felt an inner warmth that other hunters had stopped to view his kill. The feeling cooled quickly when he heard a bottle clatter into the brush. The smallest of the three men cradled a rifle as he lounged against the Blazer's hood. The other two, big and paunchy, walked toward the deer.

The surliest looking of the two spoke through a heavy beard. "My deer. I shot him early, next road over. Saw him come this way."

"My son's deer." Big Mike answered quietly. "I flushed him from the rim rock."

"Cut the palaver and load the damned thing," the scrawny one said from the Blazer. "We're outta' booze!"

"No," Michael said as he stepped forward. Big Mike restrained the boy with a firm hand on his arm, pulled him back several paces and said, "There's always another deer." Michael wanted his dad to stop the drunks, wanted the grins back.

"A good attitude," the bearded man said as they loaded the buck into the Blazer. He then locked the Hatchett pickup, throwing keys toward the water hole. Big Mike maintained his grip on Michael until the Blazer rounded a stand of trees, then set about finding his keys.

Tears are no longer an option for relief to a young man of fourteen years. Stinging eyes and a constricting throat warned Michael to concentrate on his anger instead of his loss. His stomach convulsed with the thought that his own father and chosen role model had allowed such an obscenity to happen virtually without objection. Michael picked up the keys he had almost stepped on. Still speechless, he handed them to his father and walked to the truck, pausing only to pick up his deer tag discarded by the men who had taken his buck.

A thick silence hung in the pickup cab that seemed louder than the road noise. Big Mike passed the turnoff to camp and turned onto the Izee road toward Hines and Burns, driving fast on the twisting road, much faster on several long, straight stretches. His racing mind formulated and discarded a thousand plans to retrieve the deer.

"We couldn't win back there," he said.

"We didn't try!" came the reply.

Big Mike winced, knowing that the word "we" carried the implied meaning of "you." He tried again.

"Five armed men in the woods, three of them drunk and all of them angry, leads to disaster."

"Yes, sir," Michael said quietly and without inflection but the formality placed emphasis on the wedge between them.

A white-knuckle grip on the steering wheel and an enlarged neck vein provided the only outward signs of Big Mike's perplexity and anger as he spoke deliberately. "Why did you cut those notches into that deer's hoof?"

"You always do it," his son said.

"I started doing that about your age after two men took a deer from me, much like what happened to you today," Big Mike said. "I fought for my deer and took a bad beating. I never got that deer back but we'll get yours back and take it home with us!"

They looked for the Blazer on a slow drive through Hines, then into Burns where they passed several taverns and bars without results. On the return trip to Hines, they drove through a small shopping center in an area where the two growing towns had almost merged. Not surprisingly they found the Blazer they sought standing among several vehicles parked at the front of a liquor store.

Big Mike braked the pickup to a stop and stared intently at the blazer as he reviewed his options. Perhaps he should just call the police, a safe and sensible action, but a glance at his son told him he needed a more personal solution. Big Mike had often advised his son to cultivate the manly trait of avoiding physical violence. He could grudgingly accept the loss of his own deer, but not the blatant theft of his son's first buck.

"Wait here," Big Mike said before walking to the Blazer's rear.

Michael's deer lay atop the folded down rear seat. He tried the tailgate latch and found it locked. He ducked as he turned to the sound of running feet and met the impact of the bearded man with his shoulder. A quick left jab into the thick beard did no serious damage but riveted the man's attention long enough for Big Mike to put all his strength behind a hard first that plowed deep into an overhanging paunch. Whiskey-laden breath rushed audibly through the beard as the groaning man folded on his knees.

The two companions of the bearded man came to his assistance. As Big Mike grappled with the largest of the pair, the smaller one circled threateningly, waving a full bottle of bourbon and screaming curses. Other folks began watching the entertainment. Michael left the pickup at a dead run and tackled the bottle waver, then felt a pair of sharp blows to his face just as a squeal of brakes and siren sounded.

"Knock it off. Now!" A state trooper demanded as he jerked the flailing smaller man from astride Michael. "What's going on here?"

Big Mike listened as his second antagonist accused the Hatchets of attempting a break-in of the Blazer, and then detailed an account of events as they had happened.

"You're a liar!" the boozy runt retorted. "You had never seen that deer before you tried to steal it."

"Then how," Big Mike asked, "How do I know that this deer was hit center body just behind the left front shoulder, or that he has two small 'V' notches on his right front hoof?"

"Open it," the trooper jerked a thumb toward the Blazer tailgate. "Your deer," he said to Michael and proceeded to take the marked hoof as evidence by disjointing it at the knee.

The trooper checked all licenses and then issued a summons to Justice Court for each of the five to appear in three days. As he entered his patrol car to leave, he waved his ticket book at the three Blazer riders. "When that vehicle moves from here, it had better be with a sober driver!"

The Hatchetts left the small crowd that had gathered and boarded their pickup.

"You're going to have a pretty good shiner," Big Mike said as he gently touched Michael's swollen left eye.

"It doesn't hurt too much," came the reply. "In fact, nothing hurts much now."

"We had better head for camp." Big Mike said as he turned onto the highway. "We have a good buck to hang and another tag to fill."

They enjoyed the relaxing drive back into the

trees, slower than the frenetic pace that had brought them into town. Michael turned for one long, admiring look at the buck that lay in the pickup bed, and then popped the caps on a pair of colas from the cooler at his feet. He handed one to Big Mike, watched admiringly as his father took a long pull from the beaded can, and then proceeded to drink from his own in the same fashion.

It was a quiet ride, the third silence of the day, the symphony complete.

An Experience in Hypothermia

I could not control the involuntary shivering. Teeth chattering agony seemed to permeate each fiber of my body. The all-encompassing cold that gripped me originated not from a blizzard of ice or snow but from the horizontal rain of a Pacific storm that engulfed the rugged mountains of the central Oregon coast during a November night of nineteen seventy six. The Fahrenheit thermometer that night registered a low of forty degrees. The absolute darkness of a starless sky only served to intensify the panic that threatened to engulf me. An involuntarily laugh escaped me with the irony that US 101, the premiere coastal highway, lay a scant three miles to the west. The idea that I might die so close to relative safety and at a temperature above freezing seemed ludicrous.

The day had begun on a high note of optimism as Rick Riggs and I left Fisherman's Wharf restaurant in Florence, Oregon to hunt elk. Clouds covered the sky as they do on most days from November through April on the Oregon coast. Rain persists throughout the winter months at lower elevations while snow accumulates in the mountains, a necessary weather cycle to keep Oregon green the year around. Newcomers to coastal Oregon are often surprised to learn we are a rainforest.

The hunt we had planned for that day seemed basically sound and promised a likely encounter with elk. The Rock Creek camp ground and recreation area, which lies nine miles north of Florence, Oregon on US Highway 101, is a known nighttime bedding ground for elk. While you can't hunt in the park, the Bureau of Land Management permits hunting in the public land above and to the east of the park. Rick and I would take one pickup into the timbered area above Rock Creek to a point where a north-south road parallels the beach some three miles east and three thousand feet above the park. Rick's father Ed and his brother Bobby would leave their pickup in the park and hike into stands several hundred yards above the park. If we did not sight elk on our trip down through the brush, we might push some of them ahead of us toward Ed and Bobby. If we got a bull elk, the pack would be downhill.

We had never hunted this particular spot before, but expected a hard trek. All elk hunting on the Oregon coast takes place in thick brush on steep slopes. Few hunters bring out whole Roosevelt elk but rather they quarter them and carry them out the hard way, on pack boards.

Rick and I left the forest service road to start our downhill hunt with a separation of fifty yards between us. We plunged immediately into thick undergrowth of salal, blackberry, salmonberry and dense stands of alder saplings. Overgrown and eroded logging roads crisscrossed the area. Rotting stumps of four to six feet in diameter gave mute testimony to the old growth logging that had occurred half a century before. We couldn't see each other but we knew the rule of thumb for hunting the western slope of Oregon's coastal range mountains. Position by the sun, when available, otherwise, head toward the sound of ocean surf. When confused by difficult terrain or lack of ocean noise, find flowing water and follow it downhill. Numerous creeks empty into the Pacific in this area and that means Highway 101 lay just ahead.

The State has designated a few areas in Oregon as wilderness areas, mostly in the Cascade Mountains. In the coastal range, a five minute walk from any logging road can deliver you into an area unchanged for a thousand years, with the exception that loggers have harvested the old growth trees.

Our hunt would last three to four hours. We dropped into Rock Creek at nine-thirty. We saw plentiful signs of elk and several times we had heard brush breaking but had not spotted an animal. Ed and Bobby had seen only two out-of-season deer.

Over a lunch of sandwiches and coffee, we decided to make the run again but some five hundred yards to the south and angling toward the same exit point. Ed and Bobby offered to make the second run but Rick and I thought we could come through quicker because we knew the general lay of the terrain. Those five hundred yards moved us into a different world.

The thick undergrowth of three to six feet in height now became an almost impenetrable wall of greenery that sloped toward a series of rock and clay ledges with drops of ten to thirty feet. I realized that an entire herd of elk could pass within a few feet of me without presenting a single identifiable target. My focus on the difficult terrain diverted my attention from the darkening sky and increasing wind. The storm that had built roared in from the west with a vengeance. Large, stinging drops of rain pelted my face as swirling winds whipped treetops.

Occasional game trails through the dense underbrush invariably meandered to a side hill or doubled back toward the top. Detours around sudden drop-offs and vicious thickets of matted vines cost valuable time. A glance at my watch brought the realization that our progress was losing its race with the clock. We were three hours deep into an estimated four hour run with well less than half the distance covered. I knew that I must utilize the fading daylight to prepare for a night on the slopes. I surveyed my immediate surroundings looking for an advantageous spot to den up when I spotted Rick side hilling across a narrow draw. The wind swallowed my loud call but a shot from my thirty-ought-six got his attention. We met on the leeward side of a large cedar and agreed to use what daylight remained to prepare for the night.

First we had to build a fire. A quick inventory of our assets proved them meager: two Zippo lighters and an inexhaustible supply of rain soaked wood. We dressed in denim pants and jackets, each of us thoroughly soaked. We'd left rain gear in the pickup, as the thick plastic made too much noise in the brush. Also in the pickup, my Survival Belt that consisted of a container of waterproof matches, two compact aluminum space blankets, two lengths of strong nylon cord and six two-inch cubes of pitch that would ignite a fire under the worst of conditions.

We gathered what dead wood we could find and set about whittling off the soaked outer layer hoping to find a drier interior…no such luck. I produced a plastic wrapped beef sandwich from my pocket and cut it in half.

"You eat it," Rick responded when I offered a portion to him. "I'm not hungry."

"Neither am I," I replied, "But you're the only thing I have to keep me warm and we may both need the calories."

The exercise of the hunt had kept up circulation and produced body heat. With further progress in the dark prohibited, our body heat dissipated and the chill of hypothermia began its assault. I tried to remember what I had read of the dangers in exposure. The first thing that came to mind was a woolen cap hanging in my closet once worn in cold country by my wife's father. One of the magazine articles I recalled stated that we lose up to eighty percent of body heat through our heads. Our denim clothing offered little or no insulation against the wet, penetrating cold. Like a little kid I demurred the wearing of wool as too scratchy. That same magazine article had listed wool as one of the few properties that keeps its insulating factor when wet. Amazing what you can think of in hindsight. The wind subsided a bit, giving us opportunity to gather ferns and cedar boughs for bedding. We knew we might have to wait at least ten hours for enough light to attempt walking out. Cold and aching muscles and joints demanded rest but exercise seemed our only solution to maintaining body heat.

"We can do it," I said to Rick. "We have to curl up in these ferns and conserve body heat."

Rick, a macho guy, reacted predictably to my suggestion. "I'm not gonna curl up next to a hairy-leg, yours or anyone else's." With that he flopped into the ferns.

With no further discussion, I curled up around his fetal position and hoped the shivering would subside. We didn't sleep restfully but lapses into fitful and exhausted dozing gave brief respite.

Rick's loud complaint jarred me to full consciousness. "My butt is the only part of me that ain't freezing!"

Without a reply, I flopped from my right to my left side and the macho Rick curled up around me. This flip-flop process repeated throughout the night. Rick's expressed a strong desire that our activities remain privileged information. So please don't tell anyone.

As the front of the storm plowed inland, the torrent of horizontal rain turned into a steady drizzle typical of Oregon's coast in winter. I suppose the wind-chill factor subsided but the all-encompassing cold that penetrated and engulfed me continued.

Between dozing and flip-flopping, my mind raced over the mistakes of the day: too late a start for an unfamiliar hunt; improper clothing for weather we knew could happen; and forestalling an inevitable stop to the brink of disaster. Remedial future planning included avoiding all these pitfalls but did little to relieve existing circumstances.

Somewhere between the tenth flip and the twelfth flop, I focused bleary eyes on distinguishable terrain features. I stumbled to an upright stance and stood convinced that dawn would actually occur. The rain had stopped and my world again looked survivable. Stretching, arm waving and jogging in place helped to relieve a few of the grotesque aches of a frigid night.

In the faintly gathering light, we started picking our way carefully toward the pounding surf no longer muffled by a howling wind. We had gone no more than fifty yards when we encountered a sheer face of rock and brush that might have proved catastrophic if we had pursued our course in the failing evening light. A barely accessible game trail down the drop delivered us to a giant snag fir tree that had a pitch bleed down one side. We cut resinous clumps from the old tree and ignited it easily with a Zippo lighter. The noxious fumes from that sputtering mass could not have smelled sweeter. We spent a half-hour toasting our frigid extremities, then extinguished the fire by kicking it into a puddle of rainwater.

We accomplished the hike that typical northwest November, dreary, opaque day by nursing aching joints and muscles across the difficult terrain.

We exited through Frying Pan Creek, a mile from our intended destination but on a familiar forest service road that led to US Highway 101. We walked the road no more than five minutes when Rick's grandfather picked us up. He'd patrolled the logging roads in the area all through the night. We later learned that many of our friends and neighbors had spent a long and anxious night driving forest service and logging roads, honking horns and firing rifles. We never heard a sound; our night had been as silent as it had been cold and black.

We later agreed that we were fortunate not to encounter a single hunter or searcher on our way out. If we had, they would've pronounced, "We found them!"

Hell! We weren't lost, just foolish and cold.

Nemesis

My prime antagonist, a paradoxical eight-year old, who answers to the name of Denny Wharton, lives next-door. His tender age does not lessen my respect for his adversarial potential.

Denny has many traits and mannerisms usually attributed to boys his age. Gifted with boundless energy and displaying unbridled enthusiasm for his selected endeavor of the moment, he remains a joy to most of the neighborhood. Yet, to cultivate a relationship with Denny, one courts disaster. Calamitous events occur with astonishing regularity when this otherwise likable and affable youngster stands cherubically nearby. I have often considered the lad a reincarnation of the Biblical Jonah of ill fortune. To support this unlikely theory, I recount the recent events of July twenty-fifth.

I had spent the morning tending my small vegetable garden and I bit into a sandwich, a ham and Swiss on rye at the shaded table on my patio.

Then I heard the creak of my rear gate followed by the sound of a too-familiar voice. "Whatcha' gonna' eat?"

I fought against the impulse to run to the sanctum of my house. I motioned the lad to a seat at my table and excused myself to prepare another sandwich and iced tea. I reasoned away my misgivings about the youngster as I prepared his sandwich as carefully as I had my own. Butter went onto one slice of rye bread, mustard on the other. A generous pile of thin sliced delicatessen ham, two slices of Swiss cheese and a sprinkling of shredded lettuce made up the center of my gourmet offering. After all, it wasn't little Denny's fault that mishaps occurred in his presence.

Wind failure entangled the string and tail of his kite in my television antenna. Further, good intentions allowed him to mix two partial cans of blue paint. How could he have known that one was latex and the other oil based? A perfectly normal curiosity had induced him to turn on a light switch while I spliced a wire into the circuit.

With a determination to exercise forgiveness and understanding, I carried sandwich and iced tea to the patio. Denny focused on the antics of a hummingbird while his large yellow dog vacuumed the plate that had contained my sandwich.

"I guess Goldie got hungry," Denny explained. "You can have half of my sandwich if you want it."

I had no appetite.

Denny gave occasional pinches of crust to Goldie and washed the remainder down with tea. A muffled belch voiced his satisfaction. He also provided a fitting encore to that audacious performance. As boy and dog exited my rear gate, the rusted top hinge emitted a final squeal, and then snapped. My gate sagged awkwardly in the open position and I received a single-word apology and explanation: "Oops!"

During the following week, I wavered between a desire for revenge and guilt about having such thoughts. I admonished myself that an adult, seventy years old, should have no trouble conducting a friendly relationship with a child. The unfortunate lad, guilty of nothing more than impetuosity that put him in collision with events beyond his control, should be welcomed in a neighborly spirit. I had to break the chain of unfortunate mishaps that occurred coincidentally with Denny's presence. Guiding the boy into an interesting, yet structured activity that would require thought and planning before action seemed advisable. Fishing came to mind immediately; I would teach Denny to fish!

Instruction and practice began without delay. We took to my backyard with two spinning reels on casting rods and hookless practice lures. Denny's first cast, a whirling dance of maximum effort, nearly launched the lure into earth orbit. We retrieved the lure from an apple tree as I emphasized the importance of accuracy over distance. We sat on two folding chairs in our imaginary boat and flicked the lures at target tufts of grass and small shrubs. Denny's eagerness to graduate from grass to water and actual fishing motivated him to practice long and diligently. The big day finally arrived. Denny and I motored our way to nearby Lake Mercer with my trailer-mounted boat in tow.

"You gotta' hole in your boat," Denny announced as we prepared to launch.

I explained that he had discovered a drain and not a hole and snapped a plug into the opening at floor level on the rear transom.

"Drivin' a boat must be lotsa fun," Denny observed as we set out from the dock.

I accepted his less than subtle hint and allowed him to steer the boat for a brief period. We slowed our speed to allow me to dip several buckets of water from the lake, which I used to rinse away mud we had tracked into the boat at the launching area. Denny was astonished to see me remove the drain plug. Water from the lake rushed into the boat through the drain hole but quickly reversed its flow as we resumed speed. A natural siphoning process soon removed all water from the boat and I instructed Denny in replacing and securing the drain plug.

"Seems kind of funny," Denny observed. "Makin' a hole in the boat should cause it to sink."

Not wanting to get involved in the physics of the siphoning process, I simply stated that the drain was a special type of hole.

Denny's anxiety level soared as we neared the cove I had selected for his initiation into fishing. Trolling seemed the safest technique for a novice. Trailing lures behind a slow-moving boat usually brought good results in Lake Mercer and since it required no casting, the likelihood of snarled lines or accidental hooking lessened. I noted, with gratitude, that we had progressed to the point of actually starting to fish without mishap. All tires on my pickup remained inflated and the boat still floated.

We lost the first trout when Denny attempted to boat the fish before playing it to exhaustion. Denny lost the second when he failed to set the hook and maintain a taut line. I caught two fish, then put my rod away to concentrate on coaching and boat handling.

As Denny's percentage of fish hooked to fish boated steadily improved, I congratulated myself on a successful beginning of the luckless lad's transformation to a potentially skilled angler. I watched with satisfaction as my protégé caught the eight additional fish that made up our allowable limit of five trout each.

Evidence that Denny accepted the responsibilities of a true sportsman came on our return trip to the dock. He stripped our lines of spinners and hooks, stowed them in the tackle box, and set about cleaning the boat. He removed the drain plug and dipped up several buckets of water to rinse away bits of worm bedding and debris.

After docking the boat, we went immediately to a sink and table designated for fish cleaning. Denny amused several onlookers with a blow-by-blow account of our angling experience while I cleaned the day's catch. I left the largest fish, a fourteen-inch rainbow trout, intact (minus gills and intestines) to emphasize Denny's tale of the day to his family.

I smiled inwardly at Denny's generous attempt to let me share his moment in the sun. "Taught me everything I know 'bout fishin'," he said as he jerked a thumb in my direction. The diminutive orator held the adoring, if amused, attention of his audience until one of the group asked if this was his first time to fish.

"Nope," the boy replied. "We fished all last week in the back yard but didn't catch much though, just a few bunches of grass and a couple of bushes."

Raised eyebrows emphasized the questioning eyes now focused on me. My own attention however, riveted to the gesturing arm of Denny Wharton. His grubby little hand still clutched the plug that sealed the drain hole of my boat.

I snatched the plug and urged my seventy-year-old legs to their quivering best as I hurried to my settling boat. I tried in vain to avoid thoughts of mayhem and retribution as I bailed furiously at the knee-deep water in my boat. Several nearby fishermen assisted in rescuing the craft and winching it onto its trailer.

Denny made the sage observation that, "We gotta do something 'bout that hole!"

The Physical Game

Recently I earned a conditional certificate of good health. Conditional in that my final score made allowances for my eyeglasses, arch supports, partial dentures and a regimen of medication to control blood pressure and promote prostate health. They also factored my seventy-plus years into the equation.

Prior to kick-off, I wore a hospital gown cleverly designed for maximum airflow and little-or-no resistance to peering, poking or puncturing. Evidently I won the coin toss and took the receiving position, was tapped on the knee and penalized one long-fingered probe for kicking.

The detached, professional attitude of the attending nurse gave me a clear understanding that I would score no points with passes. My ground attack fared no better as repeated running attempts had the treadmill-like result of no gain. I could make no substitutions, although I would have welcomed it since training rules had prohibited food and liquids after midnight before game day. Intensity of the engagement was manifest in that blood was drawn on several occasions. An X-rated camera filmed the entire game for instant review.

The referees granted a time out, during which the homecoming queen hooked me up to an intravenous saline solution. This procedure did nothing to slake my thirst, but I welcomed rehydration during such a grueling contest. The addition of an anesthetic drip left me still conscious but relaxed and free of anxiety. My inhibitions lowered to a point where I no longer worried that the skimpy uniform gown would gap open and reveal a vulnerability for the look-in pass. My euphoric state precluded paranoia as I viewed a numerically superior team that consisted of doctor, nurse, orderly, anesthetist, and a rally squad of two observing medical students.

My equipment included a fiendishly designed mouthpiece. The rigid apparatus locked my jaws into a yawning pose and provided a center opening for penetrating the very core of my defense. The doctor introduced a flexible cable tipped with a tiny television camera through the mouthpiece and I had an immediate and thorough understanding of the sportscaster's phrase of "up close and personal." On reflection, I believe the medical team made a substitution without my notice. As the tiny camera and flexible cable wound through the mouthpiece and curved its way through my interior defenses, it felt more like a television set on the end of a fire hose. My vocal objection to this style of play came in a series of involuntary belches. I fully expected to see a penalty flag tossed into the melee, but found none forthcoming.

My game plan had failed me; the opposition scored repeatedly during the first half.

In my younger days, I had often experienced violent physical abuse in football pile-ups, but none to equal the intrusive indignity imposed on me by the medical team that hovered over my quaking body. Early in the third quarter I learned that a colonoscopy is not a study in punctuation. I found myself at the bottom of a massive pile-up in a fetal position when they inserted the camera. My legs immediately shot out to a rigid extension that propelled my upper torso to the end of the sacrificial table and doubled an orderly over with breathing difficultly. The doctor who quarterbacked the opposition called for a time out and suggested a deeper sedation. The orderly regained his breath and mumbled about unsportsmanlike conduct. I moaned in resignation.

The quarterback peered intently at the viewing screen and made repeated passes into my secondary defense with his camera. For a brief period it appeared that my defensive efforts might bring about a swing in momentum but a strategy huddle by the opposition resulted in a change of tactics. They assisted me from the fetal position to lying on my back with knees retracted. The petite nurse that I had pictured as homecoming queen seized the flab of my mid-section and kneaded the defenses of my interior plumbing into position for an all-out scoring effort. She should have been penalized for unnecessary roughness. I steeled myself for the expected pass but they faked me out of position with deft camera handling and I felt helpless to stop the end run that iced the game.

To the opposition's credit, they didn't taunt us or celebrate wildly near the end zone. Their congratulations on a well-played game could not assuage my dejection at what I considered a humiliating defeat. I expected a fine from the league for being doped up during a game. The lone uplifting moment of the day came as my wife (herself, a one time homecoming queen) assured me that the hot water jets of our home spa would repair aching muscles and deflated ego.

It was a moral victory that I did not receive a post-season invitation to a bowl game in the form of a CAT scan, as I am claustrophobic.

Wind, Wave and Salmon

On any given summer day sport fishermen populate the Pacific waters of Oregon's central coast pursuing Silver (Coho) and King (Chinook) salmon. They value these hardy fish for their fighting ability and gourmet dining. A basic reel on a sturdy pole with two hundred yards of twenty pound monofilament line and a little bit of luck will allow even an amateur angler to challenge this salt water delicacy. This beginner's gear will not guarantee success but will at least allow the novice an introduction to a thrilling and rewarding method of sports fishing.

My first opportunity to fish for salmon came when I moved to Florence, Oregon in 1971. A few trips over the bar with newfound friends and a moderate success in fishing for salmon, permanently addicted me to the sport. I spent all of my free time during the ensuing winter months reconditioning the hull and engine of a twenty-six foot Criss Craft cabin boat. I renamed the boat Sarge, a moniker my wife had acquired during a hitch spent in the Woman's Army Corps during World

War Two.

The boat sat on a trailer in my yard during the refitting process. It looked massive. Later I learned that the sturdy looking vessel could bob like an insignificant piece of cork in the teeth of a sudden ocean storm. What seems omnipotent in fresh water lakes and streams often provides less than token resistance to the force of even a nominal Pacific storm.

I made the first few trips over the bar without mishap and availed myself of each calm day to thrill to the wild leaping of a Silver, or feel the surging tug of a King as it sounded. The highlight of my spring came when I boated a fifteen-pound Silver and a forty-seven pound King in one day. Neither of them were records, but they did qualify as substantial.

On a fateful day in July, I eased the Sarge down the Siuslaw River and bounced across a choppy shallow bar. Incoming swells broke against river flow and offered only a narrow slit of negotiable water at channel center for small boats. Incoming tide can sometimes give you the necessary water to cross a shallow bar. I exited the river one hour after slack low tide and expected to get in four or five hours of fishing before making the return at high tide.

Water conditions outside the bar seemed acceptable. Long ocean swells of four feet rolled in from the west at one-hundred yard intervals. A light wind from the northwest caused a small surface ripple, but gave no indication of the trouble ahead. We dropped fishing lines as we passed the whistle buoy at fifteen fathoms and set a northwest trolling course into the light breeze. Guests aboard the Sarge that day were Pete and Polly Peterson of Boise, Idaho, on their first salt water excursion.

We had trolled no more than five minutes when the first hook-up occurred on the port side. I reduced power and concentrated on maintaining a stable platform from which Polly could play the Silver salmon that cavorted in a series of leaps and shallow runs. Polly had played the Silver to within fifty feet of the boat when a triangular fin sliced through the water behind the tiring fish. Polly's pole bent to an exaggerated arch, then straightened with a limp line. Pete netted the forward five pounds of what had been a ten-pound silver salmon.

"He ate my fish!" Polly vehemently expressed her disappointment to the unwelcome predator.

Perhaps her invective acted as chum, for several more fins appeared near our boat. We pulled in our gear and made a northwest run to forty fathoms before slowing to resume our troll. Salmon normally go off the bite when sharks feed.

An hour of trolling produced several strikes but no fish boated. We spotted a large flock of sea gulls concentrated in an area ahead, diving and surface feeding. This kind of activity often means that baitfish are surfacing in an attempt to escape larger fish feeding from below. Strikes on two lines as we crossed the busy area indicated we had come upon such an event.

We shortly picked up a nice twenty-pound King and a seven-pound Silver. The fishing prospects looked good, but weather conditions deteriorated. A quickening wind blew directly out of the north at some fifteen knots per hour and created waves that ran at an oblique angle to the increasing westerly swells.

Prudence dictated an end to fishing and a run for the dock. We had crossed the bar just after slack low tide, which meant we had approximately six hours in which to recross at incoming high tide. The shallow Siuslaw bar made it impossible for small craft once the tide had turned and started its outward flow. I tuned the radio to a weather station and heard small craft warnings caused by steadily increasing westerly swells spawned by a distant Pacific storm. I changed to a southeasterly course to fish our way toward the bar in the event weather conditions might worsen.

The Sarge, built for power, stability, and not speed, plodded before the gathering wind. We moved at trolling speed and wallowed in the crests and troughs of the building twelve feet swells. Serious white caps showed all around and wind swept waves slammed into our stern, sending a salty spray cascading over the deck. I understood why my ancestors feared the deep. Things changed quickly out here.

A particularly large swell came in from starboard.

I reacted with a turn into the heavy water that allowed us to crest the swell, only to fall into a trough and have a wave break over the starboard stern and flood the deck. I heard the automatic bilge pump come on and knew that things grew serious.

The outlook only got worse as we viewed the Siuslaw River bar. Swells broke completely across the shallow entrance. I reduced our speed, then turned west into the swells to delay our approach and allow time to formulate a bar-crossing strategy. Pete stood by my side with a white-knuckle grip on the bridge canopy. Polly uttered not a word but solemnly loosened the laces of her heavy hiking boots and tightened the straps of her life jacket.

While considering our limited options, A Coast Guard cutter hailed us and warned if we wanted to cross, we must do it now. The skipper explained through a bullhorn that conditions would only worsen and we must cross now or travel twenty-five miles to Winchester Bay where better conditions usually prevailed but not always.

I knew we did not want two more hours of those hammering seas and decided to run Siuslaw Bar. I spun the wheel and aimed our bow at the white water of the river's outlet. The incoming swells propelled us forward in a frenzied rush, and then left us sagging in a trough until the next swell repeated the process. We approached the bar on the crest of a massive swell and my heart raced as I looked behind me to see a monstrous sneaker wave already breaking as it closed inside the bell buoy at five fathoms.

The Coast Guard cutter, which monitored our progress swung broadside behind us to lessen the likelihood of our being swamped by the onrushing wall of water. Well-timed action by the cutter's crew ironed out a survivable gap in the tumbling mass that allowed us passage over a dangerous bar and into the welcome calm of the Siuslaw river.

Polly told me that as Pete narrated our adventure to land-locked friends in Boise, Idaho, the event took on proportions to relegate the *Poseidon Adventure* to the level of a kiddie-car ride.

We had a fortunate trip. Pete and Polly returned to Boise with gourmet Salmon steaks. More importantly, we survived our failure to maintain a proper respect for the power of wind and wave. I still cross the Siuslaw bar to fish for salmon but do so with a wary eye on bar conditions and an attentive ear for weather forecasts.

Stumpy

Cool ocean breezes seemed only a memory as I entered the August oven of Oregon's high desert. A turn to the east at Bend, Oregon placed me on highway 20 and aimed at the heart of pronghorn antelope country. The acrid spice of juniper and sagebrush grew heavy on the warm air that blew in the wing windows of my pickup. My pilgrimage from the coastal town of Florence resulted from a lucky draw for an antelope tag in the annual lottery held by the Oregon Fish and Wildlife Department. Six previous failed applications had almost ended my hope of ever hunting antelope with legal sanction. The tag that lay in my wallet insured the opportunity but did not guarantee an end result. Harvesting an antelope would complete my cycle of the big four native species in Oregon of deer, elk, bear and antelope.

A yellow post-it-note that read, "Look for Stumpy in Burns" stuck to my antelope tag. While I waited for a tag many people advised that I secure the services of Stumpy as my guide. In retrospect, it seems likely they set me up as a fall guy for the local Spit and Whittle Club. They failed to warn me about some important characteristics of this highly touted guide. I did not, however, have the advantage of hindsight as I approached the town of Burns, Oregon with high expectations. I pulled into the parking lot of the Sportsman bar and Restaurant and entered the dim-lit and cool interior known as the favorite watering hole for Stumpy. Here they told me he drank in a tavern down the street today.

I found the object of my search in that tavern. All five foot and six inches of him stood tenuously balanced at the bar, as he drank his ten o'clock breakfast of two raw eggs floated in a schooner of draft beer. He stabilized a momentary imbalance with the thump of a pegged leg, not a modern prosthetic appendage of flesh colored plastic but a hand-whittled chunk of pine that could have paced the deck of a pirate ship. The image did not inspire confidence, but the fact remained that as a novice antelope hunter the apparition before me held rumored credentials as a guide.

"I need a guide," I said while maintaining a careful distance from his stein of breakfast.

"That will be twenty dollars up front," he replied before turning to look at me. "Eighty more when you get your antelope, and you will get one, even if I have to shoot it for you," he added.

The thought of that jangled bundle of nerves

actually discharging a firearm seemed unsettling at best, but I determined to secure the services of this storied guide for what could possibly be my only antelope hunt.

I fished a twenty from my wallet and laid it on the bar, but kept it secured under my palm. "Only if you promise to sober up by morning."

"Hell, I'll promise anything you want to hear but take your damned hand off that twenty or no deal!"

I let go the twenty and it immediately disappeared into a shirt pocket. "How about a steak?"

I thought that the protein might encourage recovery. He quickly assented and we exited the tavern without my noticing the ones and fives that changed hands across the bar. I was an odds-on favorite to fall victim to Stumpy's up front demands.

Our progress back to the Sportsman Bar proceeded with frequent stumbles and lurching, but was finally accomplished. I promptly ordered two sixteen-ounce T-bones and Stumpy requested a double shot of bourbon. He was a bottomless pit. Salad, beef, bourbon, potato and garlic bread methodically consumed by a man weighing no more than one hundred forty pounds and this atop the egg and brew breakfast of a half-hour earlier.

We agreed to meet back at the Sportsman for breakfast at four thirty the following day, and then drive to the Owyhee unit near the Idaho border. I experienced relief at seeing him arrive at the appointed time and felt some security in knowing the bar would not open until seven a.m. My elation didn't last long as my diminutive guide laced his pre-breakfast coffee with a pint bottle from his pocket, then ordered bacon, eggs, hashed browned potatoes and biscuits.

As we left the town of Burns, Stumpy turned to look at the thirty-ought six rifle that hung in the rack. "What are you shooting in it?"

"One hundred sixty five grain hand loads," I answered. "Zeroed in at two hundred yards."

"We need to change that to two inches high at two hundred yards. That will give you an eleven inch kill box from one-fifty to three hundred yards."

His knowledge and coherent understanding of ballistics encouraged me, but my apprehension returned as he took another pull from his pocket jug.

While not a teetotaler, I have long held that firearms in combination with alcohol creates a volatile cocktail. "Could you forego the booze until after our hunt?" I asked.

"No! You do the driving and shooting, I'll do the drinking. I will get you a shot, just be sure you haven't been drinking."

I felt that his assurance to successfully locate and stalk antelope might be Dutch courage but as a first time pronghorn hunter in unfamiliar locale on a tight schedule, I had few options.

Stumpy parried my attempts at conversation with terse replies as he scanned the distance with my prize auto-focus binoculars. "Pretty fair glasses," he said before taking another pull from his dwindling jug.

"Not much to see out there," I said.

"Spotted two bunches of pronghorns in the last twenty miles," he retorted.

That brief exchange represented a virtual repartee, coming as it did from the taciturn dwarf. I wondered why he hadn't told me about the pronghorns soon enough for me to have a look at them. In a final attempt at dialogue, I asked Stumpy if he had lost his leg during wartime service.

"Nope, I was hanging my legs off the tailgate of a pickup when the idiot driver backed into a tree and mashed it off. It's been off ever since!"

Stumpy looked rode-hard and put up wet, I guess he was nearing seventy. From a bartender I learned that he had been christened Ignacious Aaron Adamski and familiarly called Iggy before the tailgate incident. Some of the elder residents in and around the town of Burns could attest to his hunting prowess as a young man. He had a legendary capacity for alcohol but people never ridiculed him as the town drunk. I mulled these contradictions and Stumpy stared through binoculars, mile after silent mile, until he designated an exit onto a barely discernable track into the parched and rock strewn Owyhee country.

We made dry camp in a canyon by pitching our tent and unloading bedrolls and food chests. While I straightened camp around and prepared a fire pit,

Stumpy peg-legged his way over a gentle rise and dropped from sight. We had brought two five-gallon Jerry cans of water as well as two canteens and a case of soft drinks. Before leaving, Stumpy selected a new pint of bourbon from his duffel bag, picked up the binoculars and left without a canteen.

I had started our evening meal of German sausage and noodles, when Stumpy reappeared, seemingly none the worse for his peg-legged hike and holding two rattlesnakes some thirty inches in length, sans heads. He hung the snakes from a juniper limb, skinned and dressed them, then cut them into one inch pieces which he put into a marinade of oil, bourbon, water, salt, pepper, and garlic.

He placed the coffee can that contained this concoction in a cooler chest with the explanation that, "I'll fix supper tomorrow."

We put in many bumpy and bouncing miles on opening day of pronghorn season. Over long and difficult stretches, in four-wheel drive, I felt a debt of gratitude to the salesman who had sold me an auxiliary fuel tank. I had strong reservations about fried rattlesnake steaks but decided to sample what I had often heard proclaimed as an experience in gourmet dining. I had long avoided contact with rattlesnakes. Chance encounters at a safe distance, followed by hasty withdrawals represented the extent of our relationship.

The flavor and texture of the meat pleasantly

surprised me. I had heard people say that rattlesnake tasted like chicken. I found the taste more like frog's legs. During the next two days we spotted several groups of pronghorns ideally protected by the vast openness of flat and barren terrain. I considered a break from hunting on day four to reward myself with a trip into Vale, Oregon for fuel, ice and a much-needed shower. I relegated these plans to the back burner when I awakened to the smell of coffee several hours before sunrise.

"Gonna try something different," Stumpy explained as he rummaged through his duffel bag. He took out a sixteen-inch square of red cloth and folded it into his hip pocket. "If you tell anyone about what we're gonna do I will have your scalp."

At Stumpy's direction, I drove for half an hour along a faint trail we had traveled previously, the final mile accomplished without headlights. The light of a half-moon provided scant warning for the many large rocks we encountered. As we weaved our way through obstacles, Stumpy revealed his intentions. I had heard the old story that antelope, curious by nature, will come out to investigate a red flag. I had considered the proposition as ridiculous at best and akin to the category of cat bones and chicken lips voodoo. The serious look on the face of my companion warned me not to voice my opinion.

We left my pickup in the exact middle of nowhere and stumbled through the graying light for some ten minutes before reaching a shallow depression that looked about thirty feet in circumference.

"Keep it quiet," Stumpy whispered as he set about attaching the red cloth to a gnarled six foot length of Juniper limb and planting it at the rim of the depression, or buffalo wallow as he called it.

The thought crossed my mind that I quite possibly should prepare our flag-proclaimed rampart for an assault by pronghorn antelope. Again, I did not voice my thoughts.

As visibility improved with sunrise, Stumpy made frequent belly flat advances to the rim of the depression. After several surveys, he handed the binoculars to me and pointed beyond our flag. He also placed an extended index finger against pursed lips as a demand for my silence.

The sight of a dozen or more pronghorns in the distance gave me joy - out of range for my 'ought-six' but closer than any we had spotted up until then. The minute hand on my watch agonized a slow circle as the sun climbed higher and late summer desert heat engulfed us.

Ants provided the only distraction from the building heat, which seemed to prefer my legs to their nest and the wasps that had nothing better to do than assault the sweat that beaded on my face. I made numerous attempts to view our quarry but each time Stumpy foiled my efforts with a firm hand atop my head and the caution of "Not yet." Of course, he risked a glance every few minutes.

After what seemed an eternity, Stumpy hissed his instruction to me; "Come up slow and easy. The range runs about three hundred yards and there stands a good buck on the left edge of the herd. This is your shot. Now make it!"

My view of the herd was just as Stumpy had described it and the buck stood exactly where he had said. I took deliberate aim and squeezed gently on the trigger, Bingo! The thing was done. Stumpy popped to his feet, binoculars in hand, and viewed the result.

He lowered the glasses and said, "That will be eighty bucks."

Later I experienced mild shock by remembering that on two occasions Stumpy had drank water from my canteen while we waited in his buffalo wallow. Actually, it looked more like the remains of a four wheeling mud competition following an infrequent deluge of rain. Perhaps the red flag method works. Then too, perhaps the pronghorns just meandered or grazed their way into position. I will accept the net result.

Our return to the cool interior of the Sportsman in Burns was an unheralded but welcome event. As we worked our way through a pair of T-bones, I marveled that I had never thought Stumpy impaired by his liquid diet, but then again I lacked a comparative. Perhaps I never saw him completely sober. Be all that as it may, I closed our relationship as it started, with an additional twenty-dollar bill. If luck gives me another pronghorn tag at some future drawing, I will do well to secure the services of the pint-sized, pint-guzzling Stumpy.

Murphy's Law Applied

I don't consider my introduction to elk hunting in the Coastal Range Mountains an auspicious event. I left the comfort of home and hearth at four a.m. and set out on a forty-mile drive to the Roman Nose Mountain area in the company of Carol Riggs in my pickup. Carol's two grandsons, Bob and Rick, led the way in their four by four. Rain followed us all the way. As a home and building contractor I often found Oregon winter weather conditions unfavorable for work, but never too wet for hunting.

We followed the leading taillights of Rick and Bob's pickup while anticipating the encounter with elk that we knew to roam in our chosen area to hunt. Testimony flowed from Carol on past successes in the area. The nagging voice within warned me of trouble. I turned to look at the empty gun-rack that hung over the seat of my pickup and knew the reason for my misgivings. I had left home without my rifle! I had brought two thermos bottles, one filled with coffee, and the other with beef broth. I had brought ammunition, skinning knife and three granola bars, but I had left my rifle.

Though intimidated by the response I knew I'd receive, I keyed my CB radio and announced my intention to go back for that basic requirement.

Rick and Bob made no immediate response on the radio, but Carol voiced everyone's incredulity when he exclaimed, "You left your what?"

They allowed me to return and retrieve my rifle with a minimum of conversation but an almost audible aura of disbelief emanated from Carol.

We arrived two hours late at the starting point. Rick and Bob had started their hunt without us. Carol's disappointment showed only in his reticence. We entered the brush following tracks and spoor but never sighted an elk. I don't believe Carol has ever forgiven my breach of hunting etiquette. After a day of unsuccessful hunting, we agreed to meet again the following morning. At least, all agreed except Carol. The old gentleman seemed to prefer the warmth of his wood stove to the company of a hunting partner without a rifle.

We met at Wolf Creek the next morning and this time I brought all of the required paraphernalia, including my thirty-ought-six rifle. Bob would not let the embarrassment of the day before die and insisted on seeing my rifle.

"I know you can hit with that thing," he said. "I just wanted to be sure you brought it along."

The morning started with promise as we cut trail on a herd of elk shortly after sun-up. The three of us went up-slope following the animals until our encounter with them near the ridge. No horns! Not even a spike among the twenty plus elk in that herd.

We took a two-hour circuitous route back to our pickups without spotting another animal. The cold drizzle still fell and we wanted hot coffee. I uncorked a quart thermos and poured a brimming cup of clear, steaming water intended only to pre-heat the thermos. The second thermos, scheduled for beef broth yielded the same disappointment. The coffee and broth remained in my kitchen at home. The prophecy in Murphy's Law had it right: anything that can go wrong, will go wrong.

With deliberate care, I poured each of us a generous cup of hot water. We sipped slowly and in silence until Bob shattered the quiet by announcing that he wanted to change locations and make another hunt through the brush. He further said that while he had intended to go to work at noon, he could not resist hanging around just to see what would happen next.

"After leaving your rifle at home, then bringing two thermos bottles of clear water. I've just gotta' see what you have planned for an encore," he said.

We moved over a couple of ridges and fanned out to walk our way through a large patch of re-prod. Re-prod is the logger's term for young trees planted to replace harvested timber. After no more than ten minutes into the run, I topped a small rise and saw a bull elk standing at seventy yards. He stood broadside to me looking back over his rump in the direction of Bob who came through on my right. I hit him just behind the front shoulder with a one-eighty grain from my ought-six. He barely flinched, but set off on a stiff legged trot into the re-prod. I chambered another round and got off one more shot before he hid from my view.

I knew the first shot found the target but deer hunting had not prepared me for the amount of lead some elk can absorb and still keep moving.

As I approached the spot where I had last seen the elk, I heard Rick call from my left, "Over here."

I hurried to the sound of Rick's voice and found him standing over my elk wearing a big grin. It was a good, adult male with three ivory tipped points on each side of a respectable rack of horns. Either of my two shots would have proved lethal. I have since seen elk drop in their tracks from one shot of smaller caliber. Each animal seems to react differently. Murphy gave us a break; the animal had fallen close to an old logging road and lay accessible by four-wheel drive.

We dressed out the elk and delivered it to a locker for hanging, cutting and wrapping for the freezer. We only harvested one elk that season, but each of us shared equally in three hundred forty net pounds of elk that tasted better than prime beef.

Over the intervening years, I have enjoyed numerous elk and deer hunts with Bob, Rick and

Carol, but they have never outgrown their habit of looking inquiringly at the gun rack of my pickup and pouring from my thermos with an accusing smile.

Where's There's a Will

Thirteen-year-old Thomas Everett Raines, an average student in an average rural school, preferred to spend more time at fishing than at recitation. An unruly mane of red hair framed his freckled face, and his gangly limbs grew a bit long for his compact torso. His two front teeth protruded a bit out of alignment, yet his smile could light up any room he entered. He seemed to prefer solitude; still his peers sought his company

Thomas, he did not liked to be called Tom, led an uncomplicated life in Prairie City with a regimen of farm chores and school in the winter, farm chores and fishing in the summer, and a year-round schedule of church on Sunday morning, Sunday night, and Wednesday night prayer meetings. Thomas didn't do all that much praying but his father, the Baptist minister, required his attendance each and every time the meeting hall stood open. If Thomas ever beseeched a boon from the Almighty, he prayed for a way to fish Roper's Canyon without getting caught in the act.

Prairie City residents often retold tales of the giant rainbow and cutthroat trout in Roper's Canyon. The anomalous gorge began as a narrow rift in rim rock and plunged some six hundred feet over a two-mile course. A year round flow of artesian springs had long since eroded the soil and left a clear stream flowing over bare rock and gravel that ended in a deep pool of prime trout habitat. The entire system lay within the boundaries of the Roper ranch and therefore forbidden territory to all anglers.

A pioneering ancestor of the current Roper patriarch had dammed the bottom of the canyon to create a reservoir for thirsty cattle. The ancestor stocked the lake with rainbow and cutthroat trout that thrived in the clear water. At first, area residents were allowed access for fishing and recreation but several catastrophic range fires had prompted later Roper descendants to bar all public access.

Trout of eight to twelve inches schooled in the lakes and streams near Prairie City, but tales of what once had lived in Roper's Canyon stirred the vivid imagination of Thomas Everett Raines beyond bearable limits. He had surreptitiously entered the forbidden area on several occasions but each time had found access to the small lake prohibited by the presence of watchful ranch hands. Over a snow-bound winter, with agonizing slowness, he made the perfect plan. He reviewed and refined the plan as winter's snow pack melted and the greenery of spring came to life. On a Saturday in early June, he set his plan into motion.

The primitive fence of three barbed wire strands proved small challenge to Thomas, but the intervening grasslands from fence to Canyon head required quick and careful movement. He narrowly averted discovery when a rider appeared, but the boy avoided detection by flattening himself in the knee-high prairie grass that undulated in a gentle breeze. He then raced to the canyon's edge to conceal himself among outcroppings of rock.

The next stage of encroachment demanded more effort. He tucked bits of grass and weeds under the rim of his baseball cap and draped wild, smelly, blackberry vines with stickers around his shoulders, which seemed worth the discomfort. A well-timed entrance would have negated the need for stealth and camouflage but long hours of planning demanded justification through meticulous execution.

He slithered down the canyon's edge and finally viewed the object of his assault. The small lake glistened like an emerald protected by rock walls and an earthen dam. Several ringlets caused by feeding trout showed near the shoreline. No one had challenged his encroachment and his goal lay within reach.

With deliberate care, he uncoiled a monofilament line, tied on a hook and looped a night crawler behind the hook's barb. He twirled the line around his head and launched it into the trout haven below.

"And what the Sam Hill is this all about?" a resonant voice behind Thomas demanded.

The boy turned to find himself facing a stern looking man under a narrow-brimmed Stetson hat. Quick to realize that a good defense just might be a good offense, Thomas answered with a question "And who are you?"

"Jason Roper," came the reply. "And you're trespassing."

The fact that he would be taken into Prairie City on a trespassing complaint was nothing compared to dad's reaction to his trespass. He submitted meekly to transport by pickup truck, but his fertile mind spun all the while.

"Do you go to church much?" The boy asked of his captor.

"Some," the rancher replied. "Why do you ask such a question?"

"I was just thinkin' of a Bible story I read about a guy named Samson who set the tails of foxes on fire and burned up the fields of his enemies." The boy continued "I don't guess there's too many foxes or Philistines around here, but just what do you think a few cats with kerosene soaked rags tied to their tails would do to this country in the dry summer months?"

The implied possibility of a raging range fire hit the rancher like a thunderclap. He braked his pickup to a sudden stop and shouted, "Out! Get Out Now!"

Thomas exited the pickup, but had walked no more than fifty feet when the rancher pulled alongside him. "How about letting me give you a lift back to your home?" the Stetsoned man asked.

"Maybe I better walk," Thomas answered.

"I know we didn't get off to a very good start," the rancher conceded, but we could talk with each other on the trip to town."

The boy looked quizzically at the nervous rancher as he picked bits of grass and weed camouflage from his cap. "Talk about what?"

"I need to hire a young man to patrol the canyon," Jason Roper answered. "The job wouldn't pay much of a salary, but would provide a good horse and a portable radio to report trespassers or other problems. Would you want such a job?"

"Only if it includes fishin' rights," Thomas Everett Raines said as he climbed back into the pickup. "I live in the white house behind the church."

A Jewel in the Cascades

Once I found the Holy Grail of fishing.

When returning from an army assignment to Japan in 1949, I spent a fifteen-day furlough with relatives in Oregon. The contrast of seashore, forests, mountains and high desert of the state held an allure for me that has endured. I saw the marvel of the Metolius that springs from the ground as a full-blown river and the depth and clarity of beautiful Crater Lake astonished me.

After discharge, I lost no time returning to my newfound Eden. Always a fishing and hunting enthusiast, I could not resist the call of the natural beauty of Oregon. My introduction to fishing for rainbow trout in the lakes and streams of central Oregon stirred my outdoorsman's heart. Possibly my most enduring memory of trout fishing came when Doyle Hatfield and Vick Morton treated me to a week of fishing for rainbows in the Wilderness area of the High Cascades. Today's trail into tiny Lake Nash is a well-worn hiking trail, but in those days it offered only a series of intermittent blazes high on the trunks of pine trees.

Our hike into Lake Nash wound through dense pine forests, then above the timberline to a point where snow banks still existed in shadowed and sheltered spots during the month of July. My hosts suggested a generous application of mosquito repellant before approaching the snow banks. This surprised me. I soon respected this sound advice when a dense cloud of the insects boiled from icy drifts. We only spent a short time above the timberline and dropped rapidly into a virginal valley surrounded by steep slopes with snowy peaks. I paused in breathless wonder at the scene that lay before me.

A cradle of mountains nestled the lake. If I had the art of a painter as well as that of an outdoorsman, I would paint that lake. In some sense I paint every day in memory. From my vantage point, the lake shone placid, a blue-green sheet with mirror reflections of white clouds, green pine trees and snow-capped mountain peaks. I felt an indescribable humbling reverence and an overwhelming desire to explore this miracle of nature goaded me into resuming the hike.

We set about making camp in this idyllic setting. Vick Morton assembled a broken down 243 rifle and went in search of camp meat. He returned within the hour, a small spike deer draped over his shoulder and anxious for the coffee already brewing over our campfire. We didn't make a big thing about the out-of-season deer. We had selected the provisions carefully and had bacon, flour, salt, pepper, sugar, coffee, beans, rice, dried fruit and vegetables and four quart milk cartons of frozen eggs. We didn't need the deer for survival but it did improve variety and provide some gourmet dining. Vic hung the rifle in camp as a safety measure against the unlikely event of a marauding bear or big cat. We never needed it.

I wet a hook while the others set up camp. My first attempt ever at casting a fly resulted in a rainbow trout of some ten inches, which I clumsily allowed to throw the hook. I soon discovered that the eager trout tolerated almost any degree of amateurism. I had enough trout for our evening meal in one hour and had released more fish than I kept.

In addition to Doyle, Vick and myself, three other men made up our group. The six of us shared a meal of rainbow trout, beans cooked with Jalapeno chilies and mixed vegetables we packed into camp in lightweight dried packages and re-hydrated with water from the lake. We washed this down with strong coffee, then climbed into sleeping bags under a crescent moon and an array of stars that backlit the shadowy tops of tall pines, which ringed Lake Nash like guardian sentinels.

I awakened to an odor of bacon and coffee wafting through the early morning chill. We breakfasted to the music of splashing rainbows feeding on insects and larvae. I volunteered to tidy up the camp while the others launched immediately into a catch and release contest for the larger of the feeding trout. I joined them in short order and we found that fly, spinner or small lure got virtually equal results. We kept only the injured fish unlikely to survive releasing. Still, by nine o'clock we had enough for breakfast the following morning. For the evening meal we planned to have venison liver with onions and reconstituted dried mushrooms. We cleaned, lightly salted, plastic-bagged, and immersed in the cold water of an artesian spring the trout for the next day's breakfast. The praises of a breakfast of mountain trout make a wonderful hymn.

I did not think I could ever tire of challenging trout with lightweight gear but a decent respect for the sport dictated that we refrain from injuring more fish than we could consume. We concentrated most of our angling efforts in early morning and late afternoon sessions. The lone variation in our fishing schedule came when Vick Morton discovered a waterlogged raft while exploring the lake's edge opposite our campsite. The raft was an eight by ten foot grouping of logs held together by deteriorating strands of rope. He and Doyle reinforced the bindings with surplus parachute cord from camp. They planned to float over deep water and test their bottom-fishing skills with jigs and salmon eggs.

Their efforts produced a frenetic spree of line-singing, pole bending activity before the aging raft began breaking up. They ended up swimming to shore with their fishing rods in tow and a stringer with two beautiful rainbows, each of which weighed approximately five pounds. One of the fish survived to be released, the other we baked in a folding reflector oven stuffed with reconstituted mushrooms and topped with bacon strips.

The mid portions of our days we spent on hikes through the wilderness area and lazy sunning on the lake's shore followed by an invigorating swim in cold water. It was on one of these hikes that I encountered my first bear. While following a game trail, I suddenly found myself face to face with a black bear at a distance of no more than thirty feet.

I froze in position. The bear poised in mid-stride, emitted no sound but stared and sniffed intently. The animal did not display any hostile intent but neither did it seem in a hurry to leave. I've read somewhere that running away can incite a bear to pursue. I had absolutely no intention of running toward him, so I just stayed rooted in place.

"Stand perfectly still," a voice from behind me said softly, an easy suggestion to follow, as my feet seemed anchored in concrete.

After an eternity of a few seconds, a man on horseback pulled up along side me leading a pack mule. In the face of such odds, the bear turned away into dense undergrowth.

The stranger introduced himself as a biologist with the Oregon Department of Fish and Wildlife. "Bears are usually not much of a problem," he said. "The greatest danger comes if you get between an old sow and her cubs."

As it turned out, he was enroute to Lake Nash to make camp for the night. He accompanied me back to our camp and accepted our invitation to share the evening meal with us.

He attacked a generous plate with gusto. He could not have failed to recognize our entrée as venison, but he pronounced it the tastiest and most tender beef he had ever experienced. That night we swapped hunting and fishing stories and enjoyed the warmth of a good fire in pleasant company.

The week was as tranquil as the lake. We saved and cleaned our catch from the final days of fishing and packed them in knapsacks, which we immersed in the cold spring. We broke camp the following morning, strapped on the packs and started the trek out. We paused at the crest to pack snow around the fish. We planned to halt again at the first town to ice down the fifty large trout we packed out. Our families and friends relished the cold water delicacies to the last morsel.

As my final act before leaving the ridge above Lake Nash I turned for a last look at the premiere jewel in the Cascade crown. I felt a touch of sadness in departing that peaceful haven for the frenetic bustle of work-a-day life.

I have never fulfilled my vow to return to that paradise. The regimen of school, work and family delayed my return to Oregon for twenty-two years. I have since participated in the harvest of deer, elk, steelhead, salmon and several species of trout in many locations throughout the state but have always found circumstances unfavorable to revisit Lake Nash. After a lapse of more than fifty years, I am not certain that I would now risk a return trip to that Camelot of the northwest. I couldn't bear the possibility of dried needles on those majestic trees as a result of acid rain. The likely litter by tourists, or to see an oil or fuel spill glistening on those placid waters poses the ultimate obscenity.

I prefer to retain the perfect landscape canvas in my memory.

Fisherman's Wharf
Spa to Hunters, Fishermen and Accomplished Liars

US Highway 101 hugs the Pacific coast from Mexico to Canada. The busy thoroughfare crosses the Siuslaw River via drawbridge in Florence, Oregon, some three miles inland from the ocean. The business sector of Old-town lies situated along the river in a four- block stretch east of the bridge.

Several restaurants remain among the old-town businesses on Bay Street. One of these, Fisherman's Wharf, now a tourist Mecca, was once a combination bar, dance hall and eatery that catered to local loggers, commercial fishermen and sportsmen. Hunters bagged record sized elk and deer from the bar stools daily. Fisherman landed massive salmon, steelhead and rainbow trout from the booths along the walls. Hunting and fishing yarns remain the favorite topics of conversation among the silver-tongued orators that slaked their thirst at The Wharf.

The reader should find no connection with or comparison to the San Francisco emporium of epicurean delights having the same name. The Wharf of Florence in those days only dispensed adult beverages along with meat and potatoes menu specialties. Though they provided a plain bill of fare, gourmet entertainment accompanied it in the form of hunting or fishing yarns each outdone by the succeeding one. The old adage held true: "First liar doesn't stand a chance."

Some stories fell within the bounds of possibility, others, personalized versions of old folklore, others still had the ring of truth; all stood high in entertainment value. A few choice anecdotes follow.

Buck Fever

Glen, popular at The Wharf, listened to the hunting and fishing yarns appreciably but never related one of his own. Although he lived in prime black tail deer country, he had never hunted.

Many hunters extended him invitations to join deer hunting parties each year and each year Glen declined. It came as a surprise to everyone when he finally agreed to join a deer hunt. He bought a thirty-thirty lever action rifle and spent some time at target practice.

On opening day, Glen positioned himself in a stand and four hunters began working their way through a half-mile of broken cover toward him. The walking hunters flushed several deer that sped through brush and toward Glen, one a nice buck. Glen didn't fire a shot.

The four hunters arrived at Glen's location and asked if he had seen the deer. He replied that he had emptied the 30-30 but had evidently never scored a hit.

True he had emptied the weapon and the evidence lay on the ground. In the excitement of the moment he had levered seven intact cartridges out of the rifle without firing a single shot.

ෲ   ෲ   ෲ

Photographic Proof

Uncle Charley, a taciturn old gentleman of about eighty years, came daily to The Wharf to smile at the yarns and sip sour mash bourbon. A story of obvious exaggeration might bring an audible chuckle but for the most part he just smiled and made no comment. He broke his silence when the topic of conversation turned to sturgeon.

"The Siuslaw River used to have a lot of big sturgeon in it," he said. "Guys still catch a few, but not much size to 'em."

Vocal participation by the old gentleman got everyone's immediate attention. "Just how big were those sturgeon?" someone asked.

"Best one came in at over ten feet, caught it myself," Charley answered.

Questions came in rapid order, "How much did it weigh? What did you catch it on? How did you land it?"

"Pen rod and reel with forty pound test line, full of eggs, that caviar stuff. My boy swam out and gaffed it with a hay hook on a rope. Took six men to pull that fish out."

"How much did it weigh?" Someone asked the big question.

"Dunno," came the reply. "No scales around handy but we did have a camera and the picture of that fish weighed eight pounds."

ଔ   ଔ   ଔ

Bob Cat Buffoonery

The four Svenson brothers arrived at The Wharf each day in mid afternoon. The four worked as a gypo (independent) logging crew. Their day started at sun-up and finished shortly after noon. They arrived one summer day with a great thirst and loud with uncontrolled laughter.

It seems that while logging along a creek, they had come upon a young bobcat hopelessly entangled in a discarded roll of wire mesh fencing. With great difficulty, they managed to free the spitting and snarling cat and get it into a canvas tool bag. They started their drive toward The Wharf with the captive bobcat in the bed of their extended cab pickup.

On their homeward drive, they overtook and passed another gypo crew in an older model truck that sputtered and belched blue smoke from the exhaust.

In a flash of inspiration the driving brother increased speed to get far ahead of the ailing truck, then stopped and placed the canvas tool bag in a small clearing at the roads edge. He then turned off on an old logging cat-road and parked in concealment to keep watch on the bag.

The smoking truck wheezed to a stop beside the bag and one of the crew cast furtive looks in all directions before reentering the cab holding the bag by handles attached above the latch.

The Svensons followed the smoking truck down grade closely so as to keep it under surveillance. They later reported that they had little difficulty determining the exact moment the bag was opened for inspection.

ઝ ઝ ઝ

Lost

The coastal range mountains of Oregon aren't as tall as the cloud puncturing Cascades but steep and generously wooded with fir, cedar and alder trees and tangled with thick undergrowth. They present ideal conditions for a flatlander or newcomer to become disoriented, especially during elk season when drizzling winter rains hide the sun for days or even weeks at a time. Meandering logging roads seem to go to no place in particular, often poorly marked.

Two elk hunters from Mapleton, Oregon came upon a pair of hunters from neighboring Florence and stopped to swap hunting information. During their evaluation of hunting prospects, two closely spaced shots sounded in the distance. After a minute's pause, they heard another two shots.

When the bang-bang sounded a third time, one of the group commented, "This sounds like someone is lost." He then fired off a pair of answering shots.

The signal and reply process repeated several times as the distance between the shooters narrowed. At last, a lone stranger broke from the brush, disheveled and seemingly a little embarrassed.

"Are you lost?" one of the group asked.

"Ugh . . . no, not lost," came the reply. "But my son is and I am looking for him."

"Are you driving a red Ford pickup?" the group spokesman asked.

"Yes, ugh . . . that's right, a red Ford" the stranger stammered.

"Well, I spoke to your son not more than fifteen minutes ago and he is at the pickup waiting for you."

The stranger looked about nervously then in a barely audible voice queried, "Now let's see. Just where would that truck be?"

"Just follow that game trail," one of the group instructed, then chuckled as the nervous stranger quick-stepped out of sight.

೦೩ ೦೩ ೦೩

The Proper Sex

The pros and cons of doe hunting always spark lively conversation in Fisherman's Wharf. Those against the harvesting of does consider the practice taboo, looking down at the meat hunters who consume venison of the fairer forest sex. Ed Reynolds stood foremost among those who deplored the practice.

Ed likes to think of himself as a trophy hunter and longed to fill a slot in the Boone and Crockett record book. He hunted the four-point buck. He might take a three point if it had a broad span and heavy body. He found forked horns and spikes unworthy of his effort and does remained inviolable.

Jim Raines, chief among Ed's vocal opponents, vowed that doe venison tasted sweeter. Further, he stated that left unchecked, the deer population could attain near plague status. The Oregon Department of Fish and Wildlife seemed to side with Jim. Each year, they issued varying numbers of doe tags to maintain balance between deer herds and the available forage and habitat. Jim expounded upon the necessity of doe hunting at every opportunity. Not that he was evangelical about hunting does, he just enjoyed needling Ed and hearing him rave at the abominable practice.

Jim walked slowly into an almost imperceptible breeze, moving quietly and looking ahead for deer. Thin foliage concealed him when a deer stepped from the brush to browse on young saplings. The deer stood no more than fifty yards distant and seemed totally unaware of Jim's presence. He eased his rifle into position and he could see that the rack of horns made a nice spread with three points on each side. Just before Jim squeezed the trigger a shot rang out and the deer crumpled in a heap. A hunter stepped from brush some fifty feet to Jim's left and walked toward the fallen deer. The two hunters converged at the deer.

"Good shot," Jim said, more than a little surprised to see that the other hunter was Ed Reynolds. "I had a bead on him when he dropped."

Ed propped his rifle against a tree, shed a jacket and unsheathed a knife to gut the animal. Meanwhile, Jim admired the rack of horns and fine condition of the deer. The body seemed a little small but well filled out. His gaze shifted to the prime hams; something didn't look just exactly right. Just on the verge of walking away he noticed the buck didn't have some necessary equipment. He stepped to the rear of the animal. This particular deer was seriously challenged, anatomically. Jim had heard of the phenomenon before but he had never seen a doe with horns. Ed Reynolds had shot a doe.

Jim stifled the laughter that threatened to erupt from him and addressed his adversary, "Ed, this is a thoroughly mixed up deer!"

"Just what do you mean by that remark?" Ed countered.

"This prime buck of yours is a doe" Jim chortled.

A cursory inspection revealed the awful truth. "You were all set to shoot him . . . ugh, er . . . her."

"That's for sure," Jim agreed. "Shucks, I like doe meat but I wasn't aware that you do."

"With that rack of horns, how was I to know it was a doe?" Ed asked.

"Maybe the eyelashes, "Jim said. "Then too, she has rather shapely legs, and take a look at that skinny neck."

"You're near wise-cracking your way into a thumping," Ed threatened. "I had better not hear of this thing being told around."

Jim took note of Ed's giant frame and hostile eyes. "I would never tell this to anyone," he said, all the while knowing that an impossible promise.

"Good morning," A voice said. Jim and Ed had been so absorbed with the peculiar animal that they had not noticed the approach of a man who identified himself as a game warden and asked to see their hunting licenses and deer tags. The warden entered their license numbers on a note pad and turned his attention to the deer. "Nice deer," he said, and then turned to Jim. "Your deer?"

"No," Jim replied and jerked a thumb toward Ed. "He beat me to her."

"Her?" the officer queried. "That's a fine rack of horns for a three point." He moved closer to the deer as he spoke. "Good spread, nice balance, a bit small in the body but in prime condition and...well, I'll be damned! This thing is a doe!"

"I shot because of those horns," Ed blurted defensively.

"You're legal," the officer said. "I'd have taken that shot too. I've heard of this kind of thing but in twelve years on the job I've never seen it."

Jim lost all control and doubled over with laughter when he remembered that the warden's cousin published the weekly newspaper. He regained enough composure to hear the warden speaking to Ed.

"I sure would like a picture or two. If you will stand by while I get my camera from the pickup, I will help you pack your deer to the road."

Ed made one last attempt to escape his predicament. "Instead of pictures, why not just take the whole critter and leave me my tag. That way, I can get a real buck."

"Can't do that," the warden said. "Regulations! You shot it, you tag it."

Jim joined the officer as he walked toward his pickup. "You guys don't need me here and I should get back to town."

He turned for a last look at the forlorn Ed pacing nervously around the deer. He chuckled with anticipation as he aimed his pickup toward the town of Florence and the audience awaiting him at Fisherman's Wharf.

ଔ ଔ ଔ

A Whale of a Yarn

George Little came to Oregon from Cotton County, Oklahoma. When he wasn't busy pushing an eighteen-wheeler cross-country, you could find him on a barstool at Fisherman's Wharf. He stayed free of the sauce when in his truck but his thirst between hauls grew fierce. A reticent person by nature, alcohol transformed him into a man of rapier-like wit with a keen appreciation for the absurd.

Few memories of Cotton County, Oklahoma appealed to George. However, he did like fishing on Cache Creek and the Washita River. His testimonials to the denizen catfish of those streams seemed generously laced with superlatives that he truly loved to share with new comers to the Wharf. He told the tales of behemoth catfish, and then authenticated it with a snapshot showing a catfish that spanned the full length of a flatbed trailer. George manufactured this verification by posing a twelve-inch catfish on his son's toy truck. The size of the catfish featured in George's tales grew in direct proportion to the length of time he had sat on the barstool.

On a warm Saturday afternoon, George entertained at his loquacious best with his usual fare when a tourist dared to challenge his veracity.

"That picture is rigged," the tourist said. "I resent your thinking me to be so gullible!" He then insisted that George apologize by truthfully stating the exact size of the largest catfish he had caught.

"The absolute and unvarnished truth?" George asked.

"Yes!" the tourist insisted. "For once the truth."

"Okay," George agreed. "Sixteen inches."

"I am not a good fisherman," the tourist said, "but I have caught a lot of catfish that exceeded sixteen inches."

George asked, "Between the eyes?"

Fate presented George with an opportunity for the greatest fish story ever spun. He was two hundred miles from home on a return trip when a radio newscast announced that forty-one whales had beached themselves near his home in Florence, Oregon. He quickly determined to take advantage of the situation.

On his arrival at home, he grabbed his fly rod and a camera and hurried to the area where the whales lay beached. He planned to pose with a fly rod alongside one of the whales. Several hundred people gathered at the site. Newspaper, magazine and television crews mingled with scientists and curious onlookers. He had expected a raucous gathering on the beach. Instead, he found the scene one of muffled quiet. Most of the huge creatures had died, victims of their own massive weight that crushed internal organs without the buoyancy of water. The whales that still lived, struggled for breath while their eyes focused on members of the bucket brigade as they poured water over the dehydrating forms. No one could do anything else to relieve the obvious suffering.

The forgotten fly rod fell from George's hand. The camera swung unused from a strap around his neck. Without a word to anyone, George walked to the water's edge and took his place among those filling the buckets.

ಉ ಉ ಉ

A Quiet Squelch

William Sean Flynn provided a perfect counterbalance to the tale-spinners that filled the barstools in The Wharf. His deceptive reticence belied a warped sense of humor that surfaced without warning. As befitted his Irish ancestry, he had a fondness for malt beverages. Bill (William only to his mother) sipped in silence while other patrons attested to their sporting prowess. An especially imaginative yarn might rate Bill's smile, but drew no comment in defiance or support. In truth, his decorum caused no complaint so long as he imbibed only on malt beverages. A departure to refreshments containing distilled spirits invariably loosed the demon that lay just under his calm façade.

A large Golden Labrador dog often accompanied Bill on his daily rounds. The big and friendly animal responded to the appropriate, if unimaginative, name of Dog. He sat erect in the passenger seat of Bill's ancient Buick. On arriving at The Wharf, Dog dismounted through the glassless window, stretched out near the front entrance and waited patiently for Bill's return. This arrangement created no problem; everyone in the small town of Florence knew and loved the congenial beast; everyone except the bar maids at the Wharf.

On the occasions when Bill's thirst required more quenching than tap beer provided, he switched to double bourbon on the rocks. The stronger beverage had a melancholic effect on Bill, which, in turn produced a longing for the company of his favorite companion . . . Dog.

While the barmaid's attention diverted to the opposite side of the big oval bar, Bill quietly opened the front entry door and Dog entered. Bill resumed his place at the bar and gently patted the stool next to him. Dog assumed an erect perch on the stool and placed his forepaws on the bar top.

Dog shared Bill's fondness for brewed and/or distilled alcohol. The animal emitted a barely audible whine of expectation as Bill produced a small dish from his jacket and poured a generous portion of his drink into it. After a brief sniff to savor the bouquet, Dog lapped greedily until the dish shined empty and clean.

The barmaid reacted immediately. She vocalized her displeasure in shrill tones and animated gestures. Dog's presence in a restaurant violated Health Department regulations. Worse yet, it breached state liquor laws and jeopardized the bar's license. The condemnation of Bill's deportment always included retrieving his now empty glass and refusal of further service.

Unperturbed, Bill produced a pocket flask, poured a generous portion into the dish and took a long pull for himself. At this time, the barmaid pranced about in a dither and bar patrons roared in stitches. Once an agitated barmaid grasped Dog's collar in an attempt to eject him. A curled lip and rumbling growl announced Dog's determination to remain. The startled woman recoiled from the bared fangs and retreated to the safety of the back bar. Dog returned to his normal state of placidness with a pleading whine that seemed to request another serving. These episodes usually ended when an exasperated barmaid threatened to call for police assistance to eject the troublesome pair. Bill and Dog made their exit and invigorated patrons would swamp the barmaid with orders.

After one particularly inspired performance, Bill and Dog exited stage left when Bill noticed a diner accompanied by a dog, which lay beneath his table. Bill's indignation at the discrimination grew rife until he learned that the diner's companion was a seeing-eye dog permitted by law access to all public areas. The offending pair left without further ado.

Barely an hour had elapsed before Bill re-entered The Wharf's front door. He wore dark glasses, carried a white cane and held a leash in his left hand tethered to a goat.

"This is Billy, my seeing-eye-goat," Bill explained as he cane-tapped his way to the bar and requested double bourbon on the rocks.

A hushed silence filled the room as onlookers anticipated a fierce vocal eruption from the barmaid. To everyone's dismay, she served Bill's requested drink, thanked him cordially for payment and turned her attention to other patrons, as though a seeing-eye-goat on the premises happened every day.

Bill poured half of the bourbon into a dish from his jacket and placed it on the floor in front of Billy.

The goat sniffed the dish, twitched his tail and deposited a small pile of pellets on the pine floor.

The barmaid served a thoroughly confused Bill a second drink in the same attentive and polite manner as the first. He sipped from the glass slowly as the realization set in that the barmaid had upstaged his finest performance. By ignoring the bizarre, the barmaid had negated its impact. Dejected by his defeat, he dragged the recalcitrant goat to the exit. To Bill's credit, he acknowledged the young lady's adroit squelch by removing both Dog and Billy from the roster of Wharf patrons, permanently.

ෂ ෂ ෂ

Poetic License

Skilled hunters and fishermen comprised the majority among the clientele of The Wharf. In recounting their exploits, they adhered to unembellished remarkable facts. A predictable trend in conversation ensued when outdoorsmen of lesser skill felt the need to compete for center stage with a bit of embroidery on actual events. These enhancements, when related with skill and moderation, bordered the believable. The inveterate prevaricator, usually well fortified with liquid bravado, failed miserably in believability but scored high in entertainment.

The theory that one who picks up a rod or rifle automatically discards truth is not necessarily an axiom chiseled in stone. One particular Wharf client admitted that he had never harvested a trout more than sixteen inches in length or a buck having more than a three-point rack of horns.

In defense of The Wharf narrators, they have limits to their creative exploits. Not once have I listened to a tale of abduction by aliens, Sasquatch (Big Foot) encounters or sightings of Jurassic survivors in local lakes.

(Footnote: I made a recent pilgrimage to Fisherman's Wharf. I didn't see many of the old regulars and the few that remained had mellowed. They had upgraded the menu and provided courteous service. The only noise came from a muted jukebox, no raucous laughter or high jinks. Most of the conversation centered on the weather, baseball and football. With a noticeable absence of dogs and goats, business flowed evenly. The mother lode that had once made The Wharf a gold mine had played out. With a reflective sigh, I paid my check and left.)

Within Sporting Limits

I have attempted nearly every sporting activity. I have had moderate success on an amateur level with a few. With most I realized quickly that my talent is that of spectator.

As a youth, I possessed a relatively quick start but invariably trailed all participants at the finish line. While serving with the Army of occupation in Japan during the late forties, I played on a football team that competed in an all service league. I developed a faster gait when our quarterback handed me the football and I faced linemen that outweighed me by a hundred pounds. Sheer terror inspired me to a pace that I have never equaled, before or since. Bolstered by the fact that I survived that football season, I allowed myself to be talked into going out for the basketball team, although I had never played the game before. The fact that everyone else had a six to ten inch height advantage over me should have served as an omen of things to come but a silver-tongued coach pleaded his need for enough players to allow for scrimmages.

I quickly discovered that while everyone else swished points through the net from various areas of the floor, the ball I used seemed too large to fit through the hoop. Then too, I was the only guy in the showers covered with abrasions and floor burns. The other team always bumped, banged and body-slammed me without objection by the referee but a whistle greeted my every attempt at self-defense. My stint as a hoopster ended the day our coach found me poised atop a stepladder and holding a basketball above the hoop.

"And just what are you doing?" he inquired.

I responded by telling him that I was determining if the basketball could actually fit through that metal ring.

As a slow learner, I fell prey to the boxing coach who needed warm bodies to serve as sparring partners. Little did I know that I had enrolled myself in the Golden Gloves Boxing Tournament.

Only a few had entered in my weight class at our small Army Post in northern Japan. They gave me the first bout by default when my opponent got bronchitis. I won my second bout when I threw a looping glove that landed on my opponent's throat and resulted in a technical knockout. I thought the boxing thing might not be all that difficult after all. For my third and final bout in local competition I faced another duffer of about my caliber who had reached local finals by circumstances similar to my own.

We both started with a flurry of glove throwing that exhausted us by the end of round one. Three minutes under those conditions is an eternity. We filled rounds two and three with memorable wild flailings devoid of style but impressive as an example of street brawling. When the sordid affair ended the ref declared me the winner and local champion of my weight class. He had probably flipped a coin. For this I received a monogrammed jacket.

A young man who took great care not to inflict the punishment I deserved, mercifully eliminated me at the next level of competition in Tokyo. This ended my brief career as a pugilist but a final repercussion followed.

After returning home with my honorable discharge, I wore my Golden Gloves jacket to a rodeo. The penetrating stares directed at me by bull riders, bronc-busters and area rednecks prompted me to shed the jacket immediately and fold that challenging golden emblem within the lining for my walk back home. A pair of golden gloves glowed briefly through kerosene-assisted flames before disappearing into the ashes that eliminated a major hazard to my health.

I was born into a family of eight boys. Dad hunted well, so my training with rifle and shotgun began early. I grew up a life-long enthusiast of hunting and fishing and have generally considered myself proficient with either rod or gun. It posed no problem to earn expert rating with an army rifle. The satisfaction I took from the proficient handling of firearms made me the perfect target for yet another coach.

While attending college on the GI Bill, the school's rifle team coach approached me and I leaped at the opportunity to practice with the exquisitely machined target rifles furnished to the team by the Army Reserved Officers Training Corps. The team competed well in a few preliminary matches and my target marksman skills grew impressively. The coach felt it vital to the team for me to participate in the William Randolph Hearst National Rifle Tournament. I dutifully complied and turned in my best performance yet by scoring above a ninety five percent. When the meet ended, my score did not make it out of the local district. They determined eventual champions by using calipers to find the tightest grouping on the all bulls-eye targets. My deflated ego bolstered a bit when I later hunted game with some of those expert target shooters. They did not do too well when challenged by moving targets. Oh well, to each his own.

A young lady who I wanted to impress once invited me to a tennis court. I had never picked up a tennis racquet, but after all, how hard could it be to swat that little ball with such a large paddle of taut strings? Her serve whistled past my ear before I could think of reacting. She responded by dishing up gentle lobs that had me racing breathlessly and swinging wildly. I will long remember her query as we left the scene of that debacle: "…and how are you at checkers?"

My hunting and fishing talents have proven adequate to let me enjoy the seasonal harvest of nature's bounty. I spend as much time at these sports as I can spare from the work-a-day world. High school, collegiate and professional sports receive all the support I can muster while in the stands or viewing by television from the safety of my couch. I have found my niche in the granite wall of sports. Physical participation in a few, appreciation of many and realizing which of these options best suits my ability.

Finale
Magic is the Hunt

As the Indian summer of October progresses to the chill of November, the time of the hunter arrives. The summer green of maple and alder leaves has faded to yellow and brown. Isolated stands of salmon berry and blueberry bushes with leaves of gold and red provide stark contrast to the deep green of cedar and fir trees that fill the slopes of Oregon's coastal mountain range. Occasional elderberry trees, almost devoid of leaves, have bright powder-blue clusters of the tiny fruit dangling from naked branches

Autumn deer and elk hunts in western Oregon occur center stage in one of North America's premier art galleries. An early morning drive up twisting logging roads tops out with a breath-taking view of small mountain peaks jutting through valley fog like bright green islands in a sea of white.

As the morning sun removes night chill and lifts valley fog, rising thermal currents take bald and golden eagles to soaring heights only to be harried by red tailed hawks and falcons on territorial patrol. Quail and ruffled grouse flush with a whirr of wings as I approach small clearings where they feed and search for sunrays that have penetrated the forest canopy.

Throughout the day you might catch an infrequent glimpse of black bear, cougar or bobcat. Deer and elk that stand motionless in the maze of fall colors, camouflaged to near perfection, their location betrayed to most viewers only by movement. Odds and ends of logging debris offer a plentiful supply of fuel for fireplace or wood stove. Careful inspection of roadside undergrowth can reveal chanterelle, shaggy mane or chicken-of-the-woods mushrooms.

The low growth of hillsides, replanted after the harvesting of timber, sometimes allows a view of the blue Pacific, undulating from the west to end as white breakers on a rock strewn beach. A master painter with the finest of canvas and oils could only produce an expensive and inadequate portrayal of what the Great Creator allows us to view and appreciate at no cost.

I renew my pantry each year with venison, elk, fish, game birds, berries and mushrooms harvested from hillsides and valley streams. I stock my woodshed with logs taken from windfall trees and logging debris. I cannot equal the harvest that I glean from nature's larder with urban purchases. Gratefully, I take no more than my allotted share.

The quiet of night envelops the forest as I make

my homeward descent with a feeling of satisfaction and contentment. Each trip provides a treasured memory and welcome rest from the high-tech frenzy of modern life. I have harmed, disturbed or taken nothing from this primeval retreat except food for my table or fuel for my fire.

I wish for you the same.

To order additional copies of
By My Nature

Name _____

Address _____

_____

_____

$16.95 x _____ copies =   _____

Sales Tax   _____
(Texas residents add 8.25% sales tax)

Please add $3.50 postage and handling for the first book
and $1.25 for each additional book   _____

Total amount due: _____

Please send check or money order for books to:
WordWright.biz, Inc.
WordWright Business Park
46561 SH 118
Alpine, TX 79830

For a complete catalog of books,
visit our site at
http://www.WordWright.biz

Printed in the United States
42497LVS00001B/28-129